No Reserves

No Reserves

M. L. Wright

Ms. Blueberry
PUBLISHING

Copyright © 2020 by Ms. Blueberry Limited

Published by Ms. Blueberry Publishing, Ms. Blueberry Limited
Published in Hong Kong

Edited and designed by Girl Friday Productions
www.girlfridayproductions.com

Cover design: Paul Barrett
Project management: Bethany Davis
Image credits: cover illustration by Erin Wallace

ISBN (paperback): 978-988-74557-0-7
ISBN (ebook): 978-988-74557-4-5

First edition

To my sun, moon, and stars: Darren
And to all the dreamers and believers
who just need a little inspiration

CHAPTER ONE

"There's a Chinese saying of how someone selling flowers will always say theirs are more fragrant than the others'. That's not me. I'm not arrogant, but we are indeed the best. I don't need to persuade or explain why; we're simply superior. Undefeatable. That's why we've been the market leader for the past ten consecutive years. But I don't need to tell you that. I'm sure you know; *everyone knows*. I'll see you next week. I've got another meeting. Bye."

"But, ah!" Madeleine managed to mutter.

"I don't take no for an answer. And besides, why would you even say no?" she asked matter-of-factly.

"I guess so, but—"

"Great! Gladys from HR will see you in a few minutes. Bye."

Like a tornado, the head of the jewelry department stormed out of the conference room as fast as she had stormed in. It was supposed to be an interview for a specialist opening at the prestigious auction house Minos. But once it started, it dawned quickly on Madeleine, or Mad for short, that it was more of a formality. The head of the jewelry department, or the Boss, as she was infamously known in the industry, commanded the room with her overbearing manner yet lanky physique. Her pale, slender face juxtaposed jet-black-lined eyes that shot daggers when she didn't speak. Mad knew the Boss was notoriously cutthroat, a well-known bitch, who, as she described herself, was someone who didn't take no for an answer. But Mad hadn't thought the interview would be conducted in such a manner. The next thing she knew, she was signing the employment contract with Gladys from HR—exactly what the Boss expected her to do.

As Gladys checked the papers, Mad looked up at the monotonous white and black defining the walls and structured furniture of the room. The blandness and sharp lines of it all were only disrupted by the blaring yellow overhead lights and vast windows on one side of the room exposing the magnetic view of the Hong Kong central business district (CBD) skyline and harbour. The skyscrapers reflected the gleamy sun off their windows against the backdrop of the bright blue sky while the ocean twisted and sparkled and the ferries and yachts zoomed past. It was an unusually beautiful day. Mad suddenly felt a gust of air-conditioning blowing on the side of her face. Even with her trusty black cashmere cardigan on, she felt cold. Gladys finally finished looking over the paperwork and stood up to usher Mad out of the room. Mad felt as if her every movement were in slow motion and wanted desperately to knock herself out of this stupor.

What just happened?

She had initially thought she would walk into Minos with the utmost confidence and show the Boss her credentials and accomplishments. She would pretend that she was completely satisfied with her current job at a smaller auction house *but* was open to other options. That did not happen at all. But who was Mad kidding? She wanted the job. Once she left the front door of Minos's Hong Kong headquarters, the powerful humidity of the tropical summer heat hit her face and awoke her senses. As she turned a corner, she smiled and jumped up in joy! "Yes! I've won the lottery!" Ignoring the bankers and hordes of shoppers surrounding her, she stomped her feet with glee and thought of all the naysayers, her belittling clients and her soon-to-be ex-coworkers. After years of subjugation, angst, and constraint, oh how she could rub this in all their faces! She was going to work at Minos! Without considering the questioning glances of passersby, Mad clenched her hands into a celebratory fist. "The world's largest auction house!" she said out loud to herself. As a specialist in *the* jewelry department, the market leader.

Reflecting on the past few years, Mad could not recall the number of times someone had asked her which auction house she worked at, only to be given a condescending look or disappointed brush-off after she replied. It was true that the auction house she currently worked at was ranked number three in the world, but in terms of prestige, reputation, and notoriousness, it was nowhere near the largest two: Minos and D's—Minos being slightly ahead in market share this year. Nothing was handed to Mad on a silver platter, and Mad had had to claw her way up, sacrificing endless hours and fighting off tears day in and day out. Although her efforts, tenacity, and toughness had made her a junior specialist, she still couldn't earn the respect, trust, and confidence that came with working at the Big Two. Now that she had landed a job at Minos, she could reply boldly that she was indeed working at the top auction house and had been promoted to specialist, and make her parents proud.

It has always been their dream.

Mad could not believe everything had gone so smoothly; now all she had to do was climb the corporate ladder. Composing herself, Mad smoothed out her fitted black dress, readjusted her leopard-skin hobo bag, and brushed her fingers through her side-swept bangs and long straight hair. She cleared her throat and walked full steam ahead.

♦ ♦ ♦

As the alarm clock rang, Mad's weary eyes popped open. With all the excitement, she hadn't been able to sleep at all and had spent the larger part of the night tossing and turning. While she brushed her teeth, congratulatory messages from friends and family played out one by one on her chats: "Go get them!" "You know you can do it!" and a notable one from her boarding school best friend, Jacqueline, "Grab them by the nuts!" Checking herself in the mirror, Mad made sure her black blouse and fitted pencil skirt were crisp and free of wrinkles. Her makeup was minimal; just enough to cover her eye bags and conceal some blemishes. She had never been comfortable with thick eyeliner or a dark lipstick. Satisfied with her ensemble, she turned around to apply the finishing touch. Her equally sparse apartment was organised well enough that she could instantly see her black cardigan hung up on the other side of the room. Other than a neat pile of books next to her bedside table, everything else was placed inside the closet, drawers, or cabinets. She wasn't a fan of clutter. She looked down at her bed where she'd laid out a black blazer.

Should I wear a black blazer or the cardigan?

Instinctually, she walked over to the black cardigan and put it on.

The last message was from her mother. "Don't dress like a whore! It's Minos, not—"

Mad grabbed her phone before the message finished playing, threw on her black patent leather heels, and rushed out of her apartment.

Mad had prescheduled an Uber, and it was waiting for her in front of her apartment already. Normally she would hail a taxi, but she didn't want to take any chances on her first day of work. Living on Hong Kong Island, as opposed to the Kowloon side, meant that it didn't take long for Mad to arrive at the Hong Kong Convention and Exhibition Centre. Mad was glad that when her parents immigrated to Canada, they didn't sell their modest little apartment on the west side of the island. With the current sky-high real estate prices, she couldn't even afford to rent an apartment in her area.

Upon arrival, Mad looked up at the massive glass building that some said was shaped like a tortoise. Built to host the 1997 handover ceremony ending the British's colonial rule, the building hosted countless significant and historical events. Mad recalled the numerous times she had stepped inside the building as an outsider attending one of Minos's prestigious previews. How glamorous and colossal it was compared with the previews held by the auction house Mad was working at. How smart, knowledgeable, and professional everyone looked at Minos. How inferior she felt.

Today, she was walking in as one of them. Taking a deep breath, Mad pushed open the glass doors and proceeded into the exhibition halls. As she walked closer to the designated area, mutters started to become more audible until she came face-to-face with chaos.

Workers screamed at each other as paintings were moved precariously across the room. "Watch it!" a man barked at Mad.

Moving aside, Mad almost knocked a construction worker off a ladder. She looked up and saw more construction staff hammering in makeshift walls, doors, ceiling lights, and showcases. People ran around with auction catalogues and papers while nervous assistants dashed past. During all the dizzying action, Mad almost missed the security guard.

"Ma'am, where's your badge?"

Mad looked up at the ominous figure. "Badge?"

"You need a badge to enter the premises," he replied sternly.

"I was just hired a few weeks ago as a specialist for the jewelry department," Mad managed to answer more confidently.

The security guard talked into his comm, and after a few seconds of verification, his face softened, and he escorted Mad to where she was supposed to be. They entered a space with newly built plastic walls reeking of toxic chemicals; cases and cardboard boxes were piled in the centre of the room. "Welcome to the jewelry department," he said, his voice heavy with disinterest, and left abruptly.

Dust was everywhere, and without the glistening preview lighting, everything looked different.

"Not as glamourous as you thought it would be?"

Mad turned to see who had spoken. Three girls, each in jeans and a plain T-shirt, stood there looking like clones of each other.

"You must be the new specialist, Madeleine. Welcome to the department. I'm Veronica, this is Lisa and Florence. You've come at the right time. Not the best outfit to wear today, but let's go before she—"

"Hello? Where is everyone?" the Boss barked as she walked out of a room Mad hadn't noticed.

Mad followed the girls as they all scurried into the room. As she entered, she saw a few more colleagues, one vigorously typing on a computer and one with a half-eaten sandwich in his mouth. The cheap fluorescent lighting in the makeshift room further depressed the already underwhelming morning.

"Welcome to the best department in the world, Madeleine!" erupted the Boss. "I see you've met some of my staff. Veronica, Lisa, and Florence, they are the specialist trainees. If you need any help with the systems or have administrative work, just go to them." Mad saw Veronica's face twitch a little underneath her forced smile when the Boss introduced them, but it was minuscule enough that anyone could have missed it. The Boss carried on introducing her staff while each of them smiled intently back at her.

"And here we have Louis, junior specialist."

A very pale thin man stepped forward to shake Mad's hand. *Such a weak handshake,* Mad couldn't resist thinking, but before she could ponder more, the Boss was back at it.

"This is Ronald; he's a specialist like you."

Ronald gobbled up the last bite of the sandwich in his mouth and pushed Louis slightly to the side to shake Mad's hand firmly. In an accent somewhere between Cantonese and American, he said, "*You* can ask me anything if you need help. I've been a specialist for years." And he stared into Mad's eyes.

"Now!" the Boss said, breaking up the awkward scene. "Let's get to work! Prepare the display stands and stationery. Specialists, take out the jewelry from the plastic bags, and set up! Private clients are coming in this afternoon." Ever so competitive, she added, "Let's get the first bid before the other departments do."

They raced out of the room, and the whole morning was spent setting up the preview showcases. The specialist trainees cleaned and organized the premises while the specialists displayed the jewelry in each case. To bring out the color intensity of the jewels, showcases with specially designed warm incandescent lighting encased jadeite and colored-stone items such as sapphires, rubies, and emeralds. Cases with specially designed white lighting were used for colorless diamonds to enhance the whiteness and make sure that each and every facet could scintillate optimally.

The Boss inspected and reorganized each item in the cases skilfully to bring out the best in each stone. Showcase lighting was further modified to help problematic stones, such as hiding flaws that came with natural stones. Stones with cracks and fissures or that were lighter toned had a higher chance of selling without direct lighting shone on them during the preview, while stones that were too dark needed stronger lighting to soften the color.

Each lot was placed strategically in the preview room. The no reserve lots were placed at the end of the room to draw the crowd in. Used to "warm up" the sale, they also broke up a consecutive streak of lots that failed to sell and gave the auctioneer a chance to regroup and command the room again. They were not the meat of the sale, nor the bread, they were the dependable butter that held everything together, and they were essential in any successful sale.

The meat of any sale was placed in the highlight cabinets in the middle of the preview room. Used to generate news and publicity, they were the rarest and highest valued lots. More importantly, they equated to at least a third of the sale, mustering salaries for most of the people in the company. As Mad placed a pair of diamond ear studs on a display stand, she looked over at Ronald and the Boss setting up an intensely green jadeite bangle in one of the highlight showcases. Although this auction wasn't considered the largest of the year, the bangle itself was already priced at "estimate on request" with a reserve price of US$10 million.

One day I will be in charge of a highlight lot.

On some auspicious occasions, the sale could feature a collection from the most notable three Ds: death, divorce, and debt. A few years ago, Minos sold a collection of jewelry pieces from the former first lady of the Republic of China. The sale set the media ablaze and caused hysteria in the saleroom. In this sale, there happened to be a few notable pieces from a well-known deceased actress, whose family was more than willing to cash in on her celebrity.

Across the room, Mad could see the girls giggling as they tried on those lots and took selfies.

"You want to try?" Louis asked Mad.

"What? Huh!" Mad was caught off guard. She hadn't even heard Louis walk up to her.

"You could try them on if you want to," Louis repeated.

"Oh, no, no, no! I don't need to try them on," Mad stammered. "I was just thinking how fortunate it must be to get this celebrity's collection. I mean we tried to get it, but the family never even offered us a meeting."

"Of course," Louis replied. "We're Minos. Why would they even consider another auction house?"

Louis laughed, and Mad followed suit, albeit a little forced. *Yes, why would they? Why would anyone?*

It was 3:00 p.m., and the setup was almost done, but a few private clients had already started to saunter in. As if the whole company knew, even the construction workers stopped barking at each other and hushed. Any one of these special clients

9

could be a king or queen of a country or a wealthy tycoon with a bank account as large as some obscure country's GDP. And everyone's salaries depended on these few clients who could end up buying the top lots of each department's offerings.

The Boss brought in a dainty woman dressed in boyfriend jeans and a Gucci T-shirt who was carrying a Balenciaga motorcycle bag. If not for the suited bodyguards with earpieces behind her, she could have been dismissed as a no one. Except, she wasn't no one. Mad recognized her as the wife of the current *Forbes* cover. The Boss whispered as she introduced the top lots to her, occasionally making a joke and laughing a pitch higher. She trailed behind the client, recommending and cherry-picking a few trays of jewels before leading the client into a private room and hastily closing the door behind her.

Mad was mesmerized as her eyes followed the subtle interplay, like an artistic modern dance. The others stared as well, hoping to learn some strategic cooing moves from the Boss. Once it was over, they turned their attention back to their messaging and social media accounts. Ronald and Louis quickly returned to their telephone conversations, reminding clients to come to the preview. Unsure of what she should be doing, Mad started wiping each diamond in the showcase below her.

How is it that they're so dirty already?

"Excuse me, may I look at that stone?"

Mad looked up and saw a man scanning the lots in the showcase. With his head bent down, Mad could only see his dishevelled floppy hair alluding to the possibility that he might have just rolled out of bed.

Mad handed him the ring she was holding, which happened to be a modest 3-carat yellow diamond, and automatically switched on her sales mode to promote the diamond.

"This is a 3.14-carat fancy vivid yellow diamond ring; the color is spectacular! Vividly saturated diamonds are very rare and come in different qualities. This happens to be one of the best qualities I've seen in my career. Not only that, look at how well it's been cut—the fire is amazing."

In her head, Mad thanked the garden leave she had before she started this job. She'd memorized the whole jewelry catalogue, so she knew every detail of each and every lot the sale had to offer. She had to make an impression in this competitive company, and a great way to start was by knowing what to sell. Thank goodness this was one of the easier lots; some stones needed more persuading.

The man frowned, finally stood up straight, and looked at Mad with his dark brown eyes. "Don't you think it's a bit too small?" he asked cockily.

Mad could see him clearly now. He was tall and built with broad swimmer's shoulders. In his late thirties or early forties, the creases between his eyebrows showed that he probably frowned a little too often for his age. Mad didn't recognize him, nor did she know whose client he was, but he must have been important if he was allowed in the room at this time of day. She hadn't expected the man to say the diamond was too small, but she tried to read his sullen face to figure out if she should agree with him or not. She wasn't sure of what she should say to sell the stone, but something in the client's eyes gave her the courage to answer.

"It's the stone that complements the beholder and not the other way around. Size would compromise what truly makes this stone so special, don't you think?"

The client flashed a quick smile. Was it a hint of mischievousness that Mad saw in that slight moment?

11

Mad took that as an invitation to continue. "You see, colored diamonds are very rare. Yellow, green, blue, pink, but red is precious. When you see a red diamond, you wouldn't want anything to compromise its spectacular color. It glows like a pigeon's blood ruby but with the fire and lustre that only diamonds have."

"Do you have a red diamond this time?" the man interrupted.

Mad flipped through the jewelry catalogue in her head. "I'm afraid we do not."

The man looked solemnly down at the yellow diamond ring. Mad waited for him to say something, but it took a full agonizing minute before he asked, "Would you mind terribly trying this on for me?"

Mad was taken aback. Again, this was not what she had expected. However, she politely replied, "It would be my pleasure."

Mad reached her right hand out to take the ring. As the man extended his hand forward, instead of the ring shank, their fingers accidently touched. Flustered, Mad quickly jolted and tried clumsily grabbing the shank, only to be interrupted by—

"Mr. Lam! Why didn't you tell me you were here already!" The Boss nudged Mad aside and grasped hold of the man's arm.

"I didn't want to intrude on your meeting with your VIP client."

"Oh, nonsense! What are you looking at?" The Boss took a glance at the yellow diamond, disdain on her face. "These lots are not for you! Come with me!" Like an eagle snatching its prey, she stole him away.

Smooth. She just swept in and marked her territory. I must be careful.

"You'll get used to it."

It was Veronica. She'd clearly seen everything, and she wasn't the only one.

Mad looked behind her and saw Lisa and Florence giggling, while Louis and Ronald quickly turned their heads around, pretending to get back to their telephone conversations. From afar, Mad could hear the Boss giggling and telling Mr. Lam which pieces to bid on and how some were priced at a steal because some were from a certain client of hers who trusted her so much, she could price the jewels as low as she wanted. Mad looked down at the yellow diamond still in her hand and put it back carefully in the showcase.

That was too awkward of me! I need to calm down.

She continued wiping the diamonds, only looking up when she heard the Boss and Mr. Lam walk out of the private room.

As Mr. Lam stepped out of the preview room, he took a quick glance in Mad's direction before swiftly exiting.

CHAPTER TWO

It had been less than twenty-four hours, but the pandemonium had dissipated by the first day of public previews. What was left behind were temporary walls and structures displaying tens of millions' worth of luxury items and works of art. As if fairy dust were sprinkled over the venue, the whole preview showroom now glistened and sparkled, looking polished, refined, and exorbitant. Expert lighting accentuated each piece, creating the essential mood for clients to buy. Whatever did not fit the projected image was hidden in the rooms far away from the clients' view.

Thirty minutes before the preview started and the doors opened, it was customary for the president of Minos to give a pep talk. Buzzing with excitement and anticipation, all the staff convened in the large auction room. As the president climbed up the stairs to the top of the stage, silence gradually fell. "Welcome, everyone! Thank you all who flew in from around the world to help with our sale. We greatly appreciate your help and hope you are well rested and ready for another spectacular sales week. We have a very busy week with a great many lots to sell. First up is the fine wine sales from Monsieur X's private cellar; I'm sure with the department's excellent sales record, they will be opening some Cristal to celebrate afterwards! Then we have our highly anticipated modern and contemporary art evening sale, eighty lots worth two hundred million US dollars. The pressure is on, my dear Leroy! Next up is Chinese paintings, Imperial ceramics, and snuff bottles from a distinguished collector. I'm sure the team has secured the clients already *this time*?"

Nervous giggling sounded from the corner of the room, causing the president to raise his whitish eyebrows. He shot them an icy glance before continuing his speech.

"Finally, we have our luxury team—watches, handbags, and of course, the formidable jewelry sale. As usual, I'm sure I don't have to worry about you," the president said, looking straight at the Boss.

With adoring eyes, the Boss smiled confidently back at the president. She basked in the rays of envious stares.

"We've got a budget to meet and many records to break. But as usual, I know we can do it. As I always say, we are . . ."

Everyone automatically chimed in. "The best auction house in the world!"

"Now forget about your families and friends, and don't even think about romance this week. Go call your clients and sell, sell, sell!"

Just like that, specialists, administration staff, country representatives, client service officers, and helpers dispersed, and the sale week began.

Hordes of clients and spectators arrived. Many flew in from mainland China, Southeast Asia, Japan, and Korea. This was the place to be seen and heard, and Minos made sure the week was filled with cocktails, dinners, and artist seminars. Jewelry department clients were quite easily distinguishable: fancy-dressed tai tais, toting Hermès Birkin bags in all sorts of exotic skins and colors, looked for items their husbands could buy for them. Trade dealers with their calculators and loupes examined each and every stone and tried to find a few deals. Amateur jewelers sheepishly looked at each jewelry piece to figure out how they were made or even just to catch a glimpse of a designer piece (which they would never have had a chance to touch if not for being inside an auction preview). Local jewelers solicited potential clients eagerly and passed out their business cards as discreetly as possible. Loud-talking new money demanded to see the largest diamond being auctioned off this time while their PAs followed loyally behind and tried to multitask on their phones.

After viewing hours was when things became even more interesting. Mistresses of tycoons hastily walked in to choose their acquisitions while the Boss tactfully made sure they weren't the same as the wives' choices. *Forbes* listed, *Tatler* 100s, and gangsters all rolled in after the press had left and quickly shuffled into the private rooms. As long as there were bids, no one cared about the hush-hush nature.

In and out the clients went, and Mad found herself assimilating quickly into the pace of things. Working the showroom, she enthusiastically helped out anyone who wanted to view a piece or try on a piece, as long as they didn't look like someone else's client. She didn't want to make the same mistake again. Nevertheless, she was only too happy to please anyone who made eye contact with her. Her go-to lines were: "Would you like to take a look at that lot?"

17

"Would you like to try on the lot? You could try it on. I can help you try it on! Would you like a bidding form? I can help you fill it out!"

"Would you like to look at your pieces over at the viewing tables? It's more comfortable there."

"Anything else you would like to look at? I can bring it over to show you!"

However, Mad soon found out that her enthusiasm was not welcomed by the Boss. On one particular occasion, Mad invited a man to sit at one of the viewing tables. When the Boss spotted them, she pulled Mad aside and asked, "Mad, why is that guy still sitting at our viewing table?"

"He's still looking at a few pieces," Mad replied. "Is there something wrong?"

The Boss stepped closer to her and said under her breath, "*Look* at him; do you know who he is?"

Mad looked over. The client was wearing a plain grey suit and white shirt, and he was using his loupe to examine the stones. He was most likely a dealer, but Mad had no idea who he was. "No."

With a condescending tone, the Boss erupted. "Exactly! Tell him to leave the table after he's done with what he's looking at. The tables are for important clients. He should stand and view at the showcases next time."

Horrified, Mad didn't know what to say but nodded obediently. Back at Mad's previous auction house, anyone could be a potential client, and everyone was treated as one.

Gosh, things are done differently here. It's so much more exclusive . . . I guess not just anyone can afford to be a client at Minos.

The high-value lots followed the same pecking order; Mad quickly found out that they were only shown to clients that *looked like* they could afford them. Technically, anyone could see them, after all it was a public preview. Each specialist had a trick to avoid showing the highlight lots to anyone they didn't want to show them to. Either they used the oh-sorry-I've-got-to-answer-this-phone-call move, or they told the interloper that they had to make an appointment beforehand or that there were too many people in the room at the moment, so for insurance-liability reasons they would have to come back at an indefinite time.

For those who couldn't keep a straight face and lie, they avoided eye contact and ignored the client. As uncomfortable as it was, Mad found each of these options hard to deliver and had to resort to showing the lot to the client instead, despite the Boss's dismay.

Fortunately, Mad was rarely put in such a position. Generally, clients just wanted Mad to help them put on jewelry, tell them the estimates, and show them the condition reports and gemstone certificates. The reports used to include information such as the number of each stone and the approximate color and clarity. But to avoid potential lawsuits, the reports had to be as vague as possible—to the point that Mad had no idea why clients kept asking to look over them.

Throughout the days, Mad could see Ronald and Louis filling in a handful of bid forms, which gave her anxiety. Deep inside, she wasn't sure she was worthy of this job. She wanted to prove that she was hired for her specialist abilities and that she could make a valuable contribution to the team. In between clients, Mad would keep on texting and calling her clients to come to the preview or remind them to bid. Each morning, the results of each person's contribution were broadcasted at the "war room" meeting.

Before the preview started, there was a war room meeting where the team was updated on which lots were sold and which lots needed more pushing. Sold lots had an absentee bid already. The uncertain lots were the ones with telephone, online, and in-room bids; the rest of the lots were unsold. There was not much you could do to control the situation during the auction. Occasionally, the pressure from the audience in the auction room or the auctioneer could sway the outcome. But for the most part, all the work had to be done beforehand.

The ultimate goal was to sell every single lot at a respectable amount. However, the chances of a white glove sale happening was highly unlikely. Hence, in order to get as close to the goal as possible, all lots had to be covered by pushing lots that had not been sold yet and pushing prices up by increasing the number of bidders competing per lot. It was a delicate dance of interest distribution.

"Lot 3251, any bids on this?" the Boss asked.

"I've got a telephone bid," Ronald replied.

"I've got a telephone bid on this too," Louis jumped in.

"From who! Your lady clients again?"

Louis giggled.

"Miss Piggy? Hulk? Buttaface? Anyhow, make sure whoever it is bids and doesn't only chat with you."

Mad looked puzzled.

"They have a nickname for all their clients," Veronica whispered in Mad's ear. "You'll know who each is when you see them. It's actually quite obvious."

"Oh," Mad answered, bewildered.

Why make up nicknames for clients . . . isn't that unprofessional?

"My client is willing to go up to two hundred thousand Hong Kong dollars, and yours?" Ronald inquired.

"Probably one hundred eighty thousand," Louis said.

"Good, then make sure your client bids up to one eighty, so Ronald can close in at two hundred," the Boss interjected. "Ronald, remember to remind your client about the buyer's premium. I don't want any blunders on your side. Understood?"

Ronald bashfully answered, "Yes, Boss."

"Next, Lot 3252"—the Boss continued—"high-value lot . . . anyone?"

Silence.

The Boss looked around the room, cleared her throat, and said, "Well, let's get to work, then."

♢ ♢ ♢

Every moment of the day was hectic. Mad was either trying to sell a lot or calling clients to come and bid for a lot. Lunches and toilet breaks were rushed lest Mad miss a chance to sell. The only break Mad had was the telephone-bidding training, which was mandatory for all new employees.

"Remember to verify each client's name before proceeding with the telephone bidding," the instructor bellowed. "Everything will be recorded so we can go back to the tapes in case of disputes."

Mad hastily wrote down her notes with her right hand while her left hand held the sandwich she was trying to finish before the training was over.

"Never try to influence the client's desire to bid or not; that is an offense and unethical. Remember, all your conversations are recorded, and there's an auditor in the room."

"If in an unfortunate event the line is lost, let the client know beforehand that *you* will call them back, and that they should not try to call your phone.

"Any questions?"

Mad readied to run out of the room, but the instructor was not finished yet.

"Call the client services number on your landline during the sale and remember, do not panic! There are clients and media in the saleroom. Any signs of disorientation and alarm would affect the whole sale momentum."

"Remember, we are the largest auction house in the world. We're here to put on a good show!"

The whole room dispersed and rushed back to their respective preview rooms as soon as the instructor finished his last sentence.

Returning to the preview room, Mad saw the girls huddled at the office door listening to a conversation. She quietly approached and heard the Boss firmly demanding, "KYC? Do you know who she is?"

"Yes, but these are the procedures," the man in the room sheepishly answered. "I think if she could just provide some documentation."

As if the first time wasn't firm enough, the Boss snapped, "I'm sure you know where your salary comes from. If my top lot doesn't reach the full potential because you were 'thinking,' then don't say that I didn't warn you."

The man quickly walked out of the room, right after the girls hastily turned around and pretended they were on their phones checking their messages.

Mad caught a glimpse of the man. He wore an ill-fitted suit and thick lenses, and he held on to a binder of papers. From his attire, he was definitely from the back office, someone who didn't need to see clients on a day-to-day basis. His persistence showed that he was most probably one of the new hires from the finance department—someone unlucky enough to be tasked with chasing down know-your-customer documents during the sale.

Obviously, the Boss was not going to let some KYC document deter her client from bidding on one of her top lots in the sale. Everyone in the company depended on sales in all the departments to do well—their livelihood depended on it. In situations like these, as long as the buyer paid, no one would check if the KYC document was supplied beforehand. As long as the buyer didn't default, no one would get into trouble, salaries would be paid, and everything would run smoothly.

After a week of previews, Mad was physically drained the day of the sale; she practically limped to work in her heels. Passing the sleeping security guard holding a rifle, she heard a ruffle in the office.

It's probably one of those IT guys fixing the computer again.

Instead, she walked in on one of the most beautiful men she had ever seen in her life. Dirty-blond hair, defined jawbones, statuesque frame. His designer suit accentuated his perfectly chiselled body. The crisp tailored white shirt unbuttoned at the top exposed his tanned skin. He looked up from the papers he was reading and grinned broadly at Mad, flashing his flawless white teeth and strikingly blue eyes.

Mad stared at those hypnotising eyes, mesmerized by their entrancing glacier blueness. The icy coldness struck her and should have provided warning. Yet his presence radiated a warm, vibrant glow, inviting her to quell all defences and walk closer. She was in a trance.

Adonis?

With an inviting smile, he professed, "Hello, I'm Javier. Woke up at four this morning and went for a workout, but I can see I'm still too early!" He confidently reached his right hand out for a handshake.

Of course, he also had to have a sexy Latino name and accent as well. Mad couldn't respond but managed a squeak before the Boss saved her from further embarrassment.

"Javier! You're finally here! Where have you been? Seychelles? Mauritius? Or Bora Bora this time?"

Javier and the Boss gave each other air kisses before she led him into the private room to continue their conversation.

Mad could not take her eyes off them. The halo of light radiated around Javier and followed him out of the room.

Who is this gorgeous-looking man?

"You've met Javier."

Mad turned around and saw Lisa and Florence.

"Yes. Who is he?"

"Only the hottest man in the world!" Lisa burst out.

Florence chimed in. "And the most talented man! He's the youngest auctioneer in Minos history and *GQ*'s best-dressed gentleman of the past few years! Swoon!"

"At the rate he's being promoted, he's going to be the next global head of Jewelry, and the best part is, he's single!" Lisa exploded with glee.

"He only dates models, Lisa," Florence snapped haughtily. "*Blond* models."

They then heard a male voice behind them, and all three quickly turned back. Expecting to see Javier emerge from the private room, they instead saw Ronald and Louis. The girls did not hide their disappointment.

"What?" Ronald asked.

All three girls returned to their stations. There were still a few more hours of preview before the sale started, and Mad had yet to score a defining bid. She rushed outside to the showroom with her catalogue to see what other lots hadn't been sold yet.

"Mad. Mad! Psssst!"

Mad looked up and saw Jacqueline.

"Jackie! You made it!" Mad was delighted to see her best friend.

Ever since their school days, Mad had known she could always count on Jackie, no matter what. Mad had been a financial aid student in a prominent boarding school, which had made it easy for people to disregard her. However, even though Jackie came from a prestigious family in Hong Kong and hung out with the crème de la crème, Mad knew she would always have her back.

"I just arrived this morning from Paris and rushed over here to see you! You look horrendous! What happened?"

And Mad could always count on her honesty.

"I've been working nonstop this past week. It's been intense, but I love it! You must come and see what we have for sale this time."

Mad was glad Jackie had made it to the preview. She had been feeling pretty lonely and awkward ever since she started her job at Minos. She wanted to exude confidence and show everyone else that she was hired for her strengths. But truth be told, she hadn't cinched any significant bids during the preview, and she wasn't quite feeling worthy.

Mad proceeded to show Jackie around the showroom, introducing the highlights of the sale with a quavering, lacklustre voice.

Jackie could tell something was not right. "What's wrong, Mad?"

Mad let out a big sigh. "Jackie, I haven't really been feeling 100 percent, and I guess I just need to get used to this auction thing on a larger, global scale. I'm glad you are here. Thank you for coming."

"Awww, Mad! Anytime! You shouldn't doubt yourself, though. You made it all the way from having no background and experience to the largest auction house in the world! Remember your nasty ex-coworkers and how they would make you do their work while they took super long lunches and never came to work on time? Oh, and how they would make you deal with the worst clients? You've paid your dues. You belong here. I'm so proud of you, and I'm sure your parents are too. Now, you want to go grab some food before your auction? You need energy; these things can last for hours!"

"I—"

The Boss cut Mad off. "War room!"

"Who's that?" Jackie asked.

"That's the Boss."

"How intriguing. You call your boss *the Boss*? I've got to ask Frances to give me the 411 on her."

"OK, Jackie, I've got to run; please stay for the auction. I'll catch up with you when this is all over. Thanks again for coming to support me. It really means a lot."

Mad rushed off to the meeting before Jackie could even say bye.

▽　▽　▽

This war room meeting was intense. Mad could clearly see the strain on everyone's faces.

Except for Javier's. His face was perplexingly smooth, youthful, cleanly shaved, and—

"Lot 3112: we have an absentee bid on this and a few telephone bids; we should be fine." The Boss read out from a printout. "Lot 3113: a few telephone bids, and there seem to be quite a few people taking a look."

"Lot 3114. Any bids on this lot?" the Boss barked.

Silence.

Like a knight in shining armour, Javier swept in. "I'll see what I can do." All the girls in the room looked at him fondly and swooned silently.

"Next lot. We have a few telephone bids but no solid bids yet. Ronald, you must push your client up to four million five hundred thousand, OK? Louis you have to help him reach that amount. If my client doesn't see other people fighting for this lot, he won't bid. Just like last auction, OK?"

Listening to their commander, Ronald and Louis nodded earnestly in unison.

"I want everyone to be in tip-top shape. Pay attention and stay focused! Don't forget your caffeine, sugar, meds, whatever you need!"

"Ladies and gentlemen," Javier added. "Let's go put on a good show and make some records!"

"Yeah!" everyone shouted and headed out to get their telephone-bidding folders from the bids office.

"Mad, could I have a word with you?" the Boss asked before Mad reached the door.

Mad slowly turned to the Boss. She expected her to ask the inevitable.

Where are your bids?

"Mad, I have a few dealer telephone bids. All they do is listen," the Boss said. "They will never bid over my private client prices anyways. But you know, we still have to open a telephone line for them. I have a few private clients who need my absolute attention. Could you be a dear and help me with these dealers? You're not too busy, are you?"

"Of course I can do that for you!" Mad exclaimed with delight.

"Perfect! I'll let the bids office know. Thank you again, Mad. I'm glad you could help me with these."

And with that, the Boss turned her back to Mad and once again dived into her emails.

Mad rushed out of the room and darted into the bids office, overjoyed that she was useful to the team after all.

CHAPTER THREE

Mad picked up her telephone-bidding folder from the bids office and headed towards the auction room. Carrying her bag filled with pens, gummy bears, and a catalogue on her shoulder, she tried to balance her cup of coffee and check her bids at the same time. Absorbed in her task, she crashed into someone and spilled her coffee all over him. Mortified, Mad looked up at a man who strangely enough wasn't justly furious.

It was Mr. Lam.

"I'm so sorry, Mr. Lam!" Mad exclaimed.

Brushing the coffee off his white shirt, Mr. Lam replied, "No, no, no, don't worry about it. I should have gotten out of your way! I saw you coming and foolishly just stood where I was. I wasn't thinking."

"No! *I'm* so sorry. I should have looked where I was going!" Mad stumbled further while frantically looking around to see if she could find anything to help him wipe off the stain.

"Look, I've got tons of these shirts. I don't even know how many I have! Now I will always remember this one, though,"

Mr. Lam joked and flashed the same mischievous smile he gave her when they first met.

Finally allowing herself to calm down, Mad looked into Mr. Lam's eyes, which told her that he was genuinely fine. She looked at the big brown stain on his shirt again.

Mad cleared her throat. "I'm so sorry again. Do let me know if I can help you with cleaning this up or anything else."

"Well, I saw you from afar and wanted to ask you about the yellow diamond you showed me the other day."

"Oh! You want to know about the interest level?" Mad inquired.

"Uh, no, uh, just that . . ." Mr. Lam rambled. "But you know what, it's almost time for the auction, so please don't mind me."

Mad looked down at her watch and gasped.

"I'm so sorry again and do let me make it up to you after the auction!" Mad said hastily and rushed off to the auction room, leaving behind Mr. Lam and a handful of curious onlookers.

Mad ran past the ropes barring the hordes of bidders waiting to be let into the auction room. The stage and countless rows of chairs were all set and ready for the sale. The enormous two-level telephone-bidding stage stood to the side. Mad hovered in front of the first row, trying to locate her seat.

Veronica shouted, "Mad, over here!"

Mad walked over and saw that she was assigned to sit in between Veronica and Louis. Place cards showed that Lisa and Florence were to sit on Veronica's left. Ronald was placed on Louis's right and next to Ronald was the Boss, centrally seated in the middle of the first row. Other country representatives sat beside her or on the top level.

Sensing that Mad was pondering the seating arrangement, Veronica explained. "The Boss always sits in the middle, in the spotlight. When you have more high-value clients than her, then maybe you can sit in the middle as well. But for now, she is the star of the show."

Mad thought about the countless images and videos she had seen of the Boss. Each a quintessential clip where the Boss confidently held her paddle up in midair after making the final winning bid or when the auctioneer hammered down a record price as the result of the Boss's clients.

That's why all those Instagram posts, advertisements, and news articles had perfectly captured images! All they had to do was set the stage. This is why Minos is ranked number one in the world. How could any other auction house compete with such professionalism?

Ten minutes before the auction started, Security let the bidders into the auction room. Groups of dealers walked in and shook hands with each other while trying to find discreet and opportune seats. Groups of ladies walked in and sat together while chatting about what they were going to bid on. It was like a social event to be seen at. Each participant carried the ubiquitous catalogue, ready to flip through lot by lot and write notes.

The room buzzed with excitement. Javier walked into the auction room. Some clients rushed over to shake his hand and chat with him. The ladies all stared at him with longing eyes and sighed as he made his way to the rostrum. The Boss finally made her entrance, and that was the cue to quiet down and sit.

A recording of the auction's terms and conditions played in English, Mandarin, and Cantonese. Upon completion, Javier picked up his gavel, prompting the telephone bidders to pick up their phones and dial their client's number, if they had not done so yet.

"Ladies and gentlemen, my name is Javier Rodriguez. I will be your main auctioneer today. Today's sale is placed in

Hong Kong dollars. Now, without further delay, let's begin with lot 3001."

The words rolled off Javier's tongue as fast as a bullet train. "We can start with one hundred thousand, one hundred ten thousand, one hundred twenty thousand—"

"One hundred thirty thousand!" a seated bidder shouted out.

Javier replied, "I have one hundred thirty thousand; would you like one hundred forty?"

The seated bidder waved his paddle, signalling *yes*, before a telephone bidder shouted, "One hundred fifty thousand!"

Javier pointed his gavel at the telephone bidder. "Thank you, Gloria; it's with you."

Swinging her head around, Mad recognized Gloria. She was featured in many glossy magazine interviews as well as seen attending plenty of parties all around the world. Not only was she beautiful, she was also smart; she was one of the stars at Minos with a handful of top clients from China. Mad followed her on Instagram and dreamt that one day she could be like her. Commanding auction rooms with her presence, jetting off to exotic parties with her clients, and accumulating hundreds of thousands of likes with each social media post.

Then the flat screen in the back of the room flashed *Singapore 160,000.*

"We have a new online bidder at one hundred sixty thousand from Singapore. Thank you!"

Back and forth Mad watched the drama playing out between the online bidder and Gloria until the lot finally reached HK$300,000.

Smiling at the audience, Javier said, "It's still with you, Gloria. Singapore, any more bids?" He looked around the room, and after a few seconds he hammered down his gavel.

Gloria took out her paddle to show Javier and simultaneously smiled at her assistant taking photographs of her. No doubt for her future social media posts.

Javier continued. "Lot 3002, we can start at eighty thousand, eighty-five thousand, ninety thousand, ninety-five thousand, one hundred thousand, one hundred ten thousand; thank you, sir, seated in the back."

Mad knew it took a lot to be an auctioneer. You had to be confident, focused, and able to multitask. However, a good auctioneer was on a completely different level; they were of a different breed. They were born to put on a show, and Mad was mesmerized by Javier's showmanship.

The way he commanded the room with his Latino accent. Even *Lot 3002* sounded sexier coming out of his mouth. The way he looked at each bidder in the room; his eyes looked like he was talking to you, and only you. His hand gestures directed everyone's focus and held their attention. He chose who was to bask in the limelight and who was not. He was the director in this show, and he was in full control.

Are you not entertained?

Dazed, Mad almost forgot to call a client.

"Lot 3050."

Mad had a bidder on lot 3051! She grabbed her phone and quickly punched in the numbers.

Why are there so many numbers?

"Hello?" Finally someone answered the phone call.

"Hello, this is Madeleine calling from Minos. Could you please authenticate your identity?"

"Um, Adam Bayer."

"Thank you, sir. We are currently at lot 3050 and your lot is 3051. Actually, the auctioneer has just started lot 3051, the

Van Cleef and Arpels minaudière, and the auctioneer is starting at—"

"Eighty thousand, do we have eighty thousand?"

"Eighty thousand, sir; would you like to bid?"

I almost messed up!

Mad shook off her trance and quickly reminded herself to
concentrate and stop acting like a fangirl obsessing over her
high school crush. Javier was dangerous if you let him suck you
into his act.

"Eighty-five thousand with you on the telephone," Javier
pointed to the Middle East representative sitting on the upper
level of the telephone-bidding stage.

"It's eighty-five thousand; would you like to bid?" Mad
asked.

"Let's wait and see."

"Um, OK. Ninety thousand, ninety-five thousand, one
hundred thousand; would you like to bid?"

The client ignored Mad.

"One hundred ten thousand. Oh, now it's two hundred
thousand; would you like to bid?"

Silence.

"Two hundred fifty thousand, three hundred thousand.
It's still not with us. Would you like to bid, sir?" Still silence.
Mad looked at the bidding form. The client was only given one
star, meaning that he didn't have a strong buying history. The
wealthiest clients were given three stars. Obviously Mad had
none of those.

"Eight hundred thousand." Clearly, he just wanted to listen
and was not going to bid at this level.

"Any more bids at eight hundred thousand? Going once,
twice, and—"

"Bid."

"Excuse me, sir?"

"Bid."

Mad shot up her hand and yelled, "Bidding, sir!" It felt like her heart jumped out and bounced back in.

"Thank you, Mad, eight hundred fifty thousand with you." Javier gestured to Mad.

"Nine hundred thousand," the Boss snapped.

"Nine hundred thousand is not with us, sir; would you like to bid?"

"Bid."

Mad waved her paddle a little too enthusiastically as she tried to shake off her adrenaline rush.

"Nine hundred fifty thousand with you, Mad," Javier said and winked at her.

Did Javier really just wink at me?

Mad tried to ignore him and held her ground.

Mad could hear the Boss urging her client on. "Are you sure you don't want the minaudière? You know, you just need this to add to your collection. I don't want you to regret it."

After a second, the Boss raised her paddle. "One million dollars, thank you."

The whole room gasped.

"It's one million dollars with another telephone bidder; would you like to bid?" Mad dubiously asked the client.

"One million against you, Mad, what do you say?" Javier asked, grinning. He put his gavel down and folded his arms in anticipation.

"Would you like to bid, sir?" Mad asked again.

"Hmmm . . ."

Mad looked up at Javier with her paddle half-raised, trying to hold as long as possible.

Silence on the other side of the line.

Javier took his gavel. "All done? Fair warning."

People stared at Mad as she nervously tried to get an answer from Mr. Bayer. "Sir?"

"I will—"

Javier knocked down the gavel.

"—bid."

Mad's heart froze. Taking a deep breath, she reluctantly replied, "Sorry, Mr. Bayer, the lot has been hammered."

"What? I said I wanted to bid! Ask the auctioneer to reopen the bid!"

Mr. Bayer was yelling.

As Javier wrote down the Boss's paddle number, he looked up at the audible commotion on Mad's phone.

"You know who I am, right? Are you new here? Ask someone else to bid for me next time!"

As calmly as possible, Mad swallowed hard and said, "Thank you, sir, for your support." Then mechanically, she hung up the phone, as if nothing happened. Smiling defiantly, she made eye contact with Javier, signalling that the show could go on.

It was not Mad's first time telephone bidding with an angry client. All Mad could do was act as professionally as possible and continue with the auction without distracting the flow of things. She had been screamed at much worse before, and on the larger scale of things, this was nothing. At the moment, Mad needed to concentrate on the sale and show others that she could handle whatever was thrown at her.

Javier smiled back and continued. "Lot 3052, a group of signed jewelry."

The sale progressed with winning bids sprinkled among the seated, online, and telephone bidders. It came as no surprise that most of the higher value bids were placed by the Boss's clients. As if to intimidate all that dared compete with her, she threw in arrogant gestures and looks at others.

Mr. Bayer's telephone bid actually did Mad some good by forcing her to focus.

"Lot 3200, an art deco emerald and diamond necklace, by Chaumet. I can start at five million. Five million five hundred thousand. Six million. Seven million five hundred thousand. Do I hear eight million?"

This was one of the more important lots from a jewelry collector. Mad looked over at the Boss, who was on the phone.

Is she going to call out the winning bid again?

"Bidding!" bawled Ronald.

"Thank you, Ronald, eight million is with you. Next bid is eight million five hundred thousand."

An old lady in the room lifted her pen.

"Thank you, madam," Javier said, with an amused look on his face. "Eight million five hundred thousand is with you."

"Nine million, sir," Ronald countered.

Javier looked intently at the old lady in the room. She slowly lifted her pen up again.

"Nine million five hundred thousand is not with you, Ronald."

Ronald mumbled anxiously on the phone and after a few seconds lifted his paddle up again.

"Ten million is with you, Ronald."

The bewildered audience in the room started looking around to see who the old lady was and if she would bid again.

She slowly lifted her pen again.

The room echoed with a cry of *wow!*

Mad tried to get a better view of the old lady, but all she could see was her very well coiffured silver hair.

"Eleven million!"

The pen slowly but surely lifted.

"Twelve million!"

Again, the pen was raised.

"Thirteen million!"

And again.

The exchange lasted until $17 million. Each time it took slightly longer for the old lady to raise her pen and get a response from Ronald's telephone bidder.

Was she a socialite? A tai tai? Who?

With all the heads blocking her view, Mad could not see who the old lady was. She tried stretching and bending her head as far as possible but to no avail. Giving up, Mad snapped her head back to see how Ronald was holding up.

It was a fairly quick movement and hard to catch. Mad wasn't sure, but had she just seen Ronald give the Boss a little tap on her thigh under the table? Neither of their heads moved as they gazed at the auction room. As Mad thought about the action that she just witnessed, Ronald shouted out "Eighteen million" confidently. Everyone clapped in the room with excitement.

Mad turned her head back to the old lady and waited for her response. It seemed like an eternity, but lo and behold, she slowly lifted her pen up again, and everyone cheered in the room.

Ending the commotion, the Boss interjected, "Nineteen million." Everyone turned to look. They clapped and cheered even louder realizing who had just stepped into the ring.

With the buyer's premium, the necklace is already selling more than twice the lower estimate!

"A new telephone bidder! Thank you! Ronald, any more bids from you?"

Ronald swiftly shook his head, and all eyes turned to the old lady.

She did not move.

Javier looked at the old lady and said, "Nineteen million is not with you, madam. It's with the telephone bidder; would you like to bid?"

The old lady slowly looked up, and to Javier's amusement raised her pen again.

Mad peered over at the Boss as she raised her paddle. The commotion in the room increased in volume.

The price is already more than the high estimate.

The old lady slowly raised her pen, to everyone's astonishment.

"Twenty million five hundred thousand! Thank you!"

The Boss talked quickly on the phone this time with her right hand covering the mouthpiece.

Mad tried to eavesdrop and heard: ". . . are you really going to let an old lady take this necklace from you? Come on, you're going to become a joke. Let's shut her down . . ."

"I must hurry you. We still have more lots to go!" Javier urged.

The old lady motioned Javier to hammer down the lot by flapping her hands in a downward motion. The enthusiastic audience in the room all started chanting *hammer* at the same time, before the Boss finally swung her paddle up for another bid and shouted, "Twenty-one million!"

Uproar ensued.

"Twenty-one million! Thank you! What say you, madam?"

Mad couldn't see the old lady's facial expression, but whatever it was, she made Javier confidently hammer down his gavel.

In unison, the whole room clapped their hands, cheering on the winning bid.

Someone in the room shrieked with joy, prompting some laughter among the seated.

"It's the vendor. Look at that smile on his face," Veronica exclaimed.

Composed, the Boss hung up the phone and flung her paddle up in victory.

This was just the beginning of a series of highlight lots and a preview of what was to come. Each lot was sprinkled with excitement and astonishment when record prices were hit—mostly made by the Boss and hammered down by Javier's "Thank you, I see we have reached a record price." It was as if a broken record played repeatedly with applause and exuberance erupting from the audience. They did say that an auction was like a show that titillated the senses and entertained the masses.

If this sort of atmosphere couldn't entice and sell, I don't know what kind of atmosphere could.

Mad had one more bid with an overseas dealer. Five lots beforehand, she dutifully called the number, careful not to miss any digits.

After a few long seconds, the voice mail played. Mad left a message, then dialled again. It went to voice mail, and Mad left a second message.

Again Mad tried the number. Her face was beginning to burn with nervousness. She dialled the numbers faster this time and reached the voice mail again. "Hello, sir, this is

Madeleine calling from Minos. It is now lot 3290 and your lot 3292 is coming up very soon. I shall call you again! Thank you!"

Soon the next lot was 3292. Mad dialled the numbers frantically this time.

"Lot 3292, a Burmese pigeon's blood ruby and diamond ring. I can start with three million," Javier announced.

"Hello?"

Finally, someone picked up!

"Hello, sir, this is Madeleine calling from Minos, your lot is starting now, and we are at three million dollars. Would you like to bid?" Mad said in one breath.

"I can't hear you. Can you hear me? I need to get better reception; wait please," the client said at the ill-timed moment.

"Hello? Hello?" Mad asked desperately.

"Five million. Any more bids?" Javier asked.

Unsure of what to do, Mad held her paddle halfway up. She called out "A minute, sir," hoping that she would be able to delay the inevitable a little longer.

All eyes were on Mad as Javier looked steadily at her.

"Hello, sir?"

Mad couldn't hear what the client said. Only static.

"I've got to hurry you, Mad," said Javier.

"Hello?"

More static.

Out of the blue, Mad heard someone in the crowd shout out, "Bidding!" She looked back and discovered it was Jackie.

"Thank you, madam, five million five hundred thousand is with you."

Miraculously, the reception resolved itself. "What is the bid now?" the client asked.

"Five million five hundred thousand dollars, sir; would you like to bid?"

"Oh, it's over what I thought it would be. No, it's OK. Thank you." He hung up.

"No more bids, thank you all!" Javier hammered the gavel down at five million five hundred thousand.

Mad's cell phone buzzed with a message. It was from Jackie.

Jackie:

> In case your client missed the lot, I can sell it to him.

Mad looked over at Jackie and mouthed, "Thank you." Jackie gave her a wink and quietly walked out of the room with her flowy dress trailing behind her, her necklaces, bracelets, and earrings clinging and clanging away.

"Is that your client?" Veronica asked.

"Yes. She's more of a friend."

"Well, she's a very rich friend."

"Lot 3293, a fancy vivid pink diamond ring."

The last lot.

A video played on the flat screen showing how the exceptional diamond was found in South Africa. Javier's distinguishable voice narrated the video. He spoke about the diamond being a gift from Mother Nature. He explained the faultless expertise that went into cutting the stone and the master craftmanship that completed the ring. The last scene showed a model wearing the ring in a magnificent glitzy ballroom filled with chandeliers and Renaissance-like oil paintings hanging in the background. A closeup showed her gently placing her hand on a man's shoulder. Panning out, you saw the man was Javier, and he ended the video saying, "The diamond is not just any stone, it's an art piece."

It's true, aside from the glitz and glamour that goes with it, these stones ultimately are all one-of-a-kind art pieces and should be appreciated as such.

The telephone bidders were all ready to bid for this rare treasure. The Boss, Ronald, Louis, and a few other country representatives were already talking to their respective clients on the phones, prepping and heightening their enthusiasm. Mad had no bids, but she sat looking as composed and confident as ever.

"I can start at two hundred ten million."

Louis shot his hand up. "Bidding!"

"Thank you, Louis. Two hundred ten million is with you."

There was a moment of silence, then the Taiwan representative lifted her paddle while still talking on the phone.

"Two hundred twenty million."

Louis waved his paddle anxiously.

"Two hundred thirty million."

The audience shifted their heads towards the Taiwan representative as she continued talking ceaselessly on the phone.

Javier put his gavel down and smiled intently at her.

The New York representative raised his paddle.

Veronica whispered in Mad's ear, "Must be a diamond dealer."

"Two hundred forty million."

Louis shook his head and put his paddle down.

The Taiwan representative continued talking on the phone.

A moment passed, and Ronald raised his finger, "Bidding, sir. Two hundred fifty million."

The New York representative raised his paddle. "Two hundred sixty million."

"Two hundred seventy million," Ronald countered.

The New York representative mumbled on the phone and took out his calculator.

Most probably calculating the price per carat including the buyer's premium for his client.

Javier continued with his alluring smile and waited patiently for the New York representative.

"Two hundred eighty million."

Once again, the excited audience clapped attentively in the room. The press at the back swung their camera lenses at Ronald, waiting for his next move.

Ronald smiled and raised his index finger again. "Two hundred ninety million."

"Whoa!" reverberated throughout the room. They then turned their heads straight towards the New York representative. Ronald dropped his finger.

Did he just tap the Boss under the table?

Mad wasn't sure. Was that intentional? Did Mad imagine it?

"Three hundred million, thank you, sir!" Mad twisted her head back towards the New York representative.

Javier looked at Ronald to see if he would reclaim the lead.

Suddenly, the Boss swung her hand up and barked out, "Bidding!"

"Three hundred ten million." Cheers erupted.

The New York representative talked even faster on the phone.

It seemed like the battle was about to end. But that was when Mad clearly saw the Boss tap Ronald's thigh under the table!

"I must hurry you; I do have a plane to catch!"

Everyone laughed at Javier's joke.

Ronald shot his hand up. "Bidding!"

"Three hundred twenty million! Thank you, Ronald."

The audience gazed in unison at the Boss, then the New York representative, who looked a little defeated.

The Boss smirked and replied, "Bidding!"

"Three hundred thirty million!"

"Wow!" echoed throughout the room.

"Any more bids? Fair warning." Javier held his hands out while he surveyed the room. "All done," he pronounced, and bang went the gavel.

Everyone clapped as the Boss victoriously raised her paddle to show Javier the winning number. All camera lenses gravitated towards her.

Mad didn't even realize she was holding her breath until she exhaled a sigh of relief. The auction was over, and from the wild reaction, it seemed like it was another record sale.

Javier looked up from the rostrum and shouted, "Ninety-five million US dollars, great job, everyone!" The Boss was quickly surrounded by top management, congratulating her on her sale, and the press waited for her to say a few words.

It was indeed another record sale.

All the telephone bidders threw their hands up and erupted in elation. Mad robotically joined in the hugging, but after eight hours of continual bidding, all she wanted to do was head home to her bed. If she had any questions about the ambiguous interplay between the Boss and Ronald, she was too tired to think about it, nor did she want to. Her parents always told her to listen more before you speak, and Mad was only too happy to do that this time. Physically, the whole week had taken a toll, and she was just glad she could return home "early" tonight and pass out.

They probably accidently tapped each other on the thigh. Minos is such a world-renowned auction house with auditors and such a great reputation. Nothing fishy could have happened.

Mad kept replaying what she had seen in her head and repeating the explanation to herself. Exhausted and drained, she fell asleep instantly on her bed after she returned home.

CHAPTER FOUR

Fully rested, Mad woke up the next day from her deep slumber only a few minutes before her alarm rang. She looked at her cell phone and promptly saw an onslaught of messages congratulating her on the record-breaking sale. She opened her Instagram account and scrolled through the posts and stories. They were mostly about the record prices and interviews that the Boss conducted after the sale. The marketing department had already posted a looped replay of the moment the Boss made the final winning bid on Instagram.

"Yes, ninety-five million US dollars is another record sale. And I couldn't have beaten our competitor again if it was not for my team and the support we have from all our clients."

Mad sighed as she put her phone down. She looked at the light seeping through her curtains, following it to the pile of clothes, the bag, and the shoes she had thrown on the floor last night. She had been too tired to organize them before she slept. Mentally, she placed the clothes in her laundry basket, shoes on her shoe rack, and bag on her desk. She looked at the rectangular box of a closet in front of her and thought about what to wear for the day. She looked at her bathroom door, envisioning the neatly placed bottles, jars, and makeup brushes, and ran through her morning routine. The image of Ronald and the Boss tapping each other's thigh crept into her head, disrupting her thoughts.

Were they fixing the prices?

Her alarm rang, stunning her.

Time to get up and get ready for the day.

Before she left her apartment, she studied herself in the mirror. Black midi dress, black cardigan, black heels; she was ready for the day. Taking her trusty prescheduled Uber, Mad walked into the office a good thirty minutes earlier than the opening time. However, she was surprised to see that most people were already at work and hectically running around. It was even more chaotic than at the convention centre! People were unpacking boxes and blocking the hallways. As Mad walked through the gallery lobby, she saw the client services department preparing the tables, sofas, and food and beverage bar for the hordes of clients that would be coming to pay and to obtain their purchased lots.

Mad reached her department and was in the process of knocking on the door when Veronica opened it.

"You're late; we have to get to work an hour earlier the day post sale."

What? No one told me.

Mad followed Veronica in. Indeed, the whole team was at work, but even more shocking, the whole office was an apocalyptic mess. It looked like a party box exploded and a myriad of catalogues, magazines, jewelry books, junk food, display stands, folders, binders, pens and pencils, cartoonish paraphernalia, mirrors, plastic bags, and other miscellaneous items covered every available surface.

"Here's your seat and your key card," Veronica said. "We have a buyers and vendor meeting in two minutes. Hopefully we can finish before clients start collecting their lots."

Mad looked at her cubicle surrounded by white walls. The neat white tabletop with a standard black computer and black office chair hadn't been touched by the chaos—yet.

Mad placed her bag on her desk. Carrying a notepad to jot down notes, she hurried towards the back of the room, careful not to bump into a precariously placed table of gemstone-testing machines and tools.

By the time she got there, the team was seated, even the Boss, at a small round table, covered with a vast array of junk food.

"Good job, everyone! Once again, we've passed our budget and beaten D's. I'm very pleased with each team member's contribution this time. I don't think there is much to improve, just keep on doing what you are doing right now."

For real? No improvements needed? There must be a catch.

"Let's go through the buyers list quickly. Then I want all of you to follow up with your client payments and start finding consignments for our next sale."

Going through the buyers list was essentially just going through each lot, naming the client who bought the lot and whose client it was. As expected, most of the successful clients belonged to the Boss, and she made sure everyone knew it. Occasionally Ronald's name or a country representative would pop up, but not very often.

"'Ruby and diamond ring. Jacqueline Fu.' Whose client is this?"

Mad quickly replied. "She's my friend, and I'm sure she will pay on time. I'll follow up with her."

The Boss looked at Mad and smiled. "OK, great." Then she said sternly to Veronica, "Make sure she's noted as a jewelry client in the system. Put Mad as the point of contact."

Mad smiled.

I have a client under my name in the system!

The girls and Ronald all gave Mad the side-eye.

Before they could finish the buyers list, a call from the front desk interrupted them. They were informed of clients who were there to pay and pick up their lot.

"Veronica, please show Mad the ropes," the Boss said before heading into her office.

Mad looked at Veronica. "Thanks, Veronica. Do let me know what I can do to help."

Veronica cast her an icy look and instructed Mad to follow her. They reached the end of a hallway where a room structured like an impenetrable safe stood.

"This is called the panic room; it's where all the jewelry is kept. The front desk will let us know when a client is here to pick up a lot. Pick up the jewelry and pouches here, go to the gallery, collect the release papers, bring the client to a room, release the lot, and sign the papers. Here you go, lot 3050. Good luck."

Veronica handed her a tray with the jewelry and pouches, turned around, and left Mad to fend for herself.

"Veronica, wait; when you are free, could you perhaps go through the terms and conditions for getting consignments?"

"Why don't you deal with releasing the lots first!" Veronica snorted and left.

What was that? When did Veronica become so hostile?

Mad looked on in utter disbelief and headed down to the gallery with her tray. As she descended the stairs, the noise escalated. At first, she thought she heard stern voices, but as she got closer, she was certain people were shouting at each other.

"Has the client paid yet?"

"I need a room right now! Do you know who my client is?"

"Can you do this a bit faster? The client is already here!"

"This isn't the lot I wanted! Go get lot 4506, not 4560!"

People perilously ran across the room with Ming dynasty vases, Monet paintings, Patek Philippe watches, Hermès handbags. Other colleagues sprinted with cardboard, bubble paper, masking tape, and alarmingly large scissors. Someone pushing a cart with a statue of a Chinese deity hollered at Mad to "Kindly move over, please." Mad moved to the side of the room, overwhelmed and clueless. Suddenly, someone tapped her on the shoulder.

"Hey, you look terribly lost. Do you need help?"

Mad looked around and saw a girl with extremely long black hair. She wore a knee-length light pink Chinese *qipao* embroidered with plum blossoms on the front. She had a notepad in one hand and her phone in the other.

"Yes, I have an item to release, but I'm not sure how to navigate around here."

"OK, line up over there at the front desk and ask for the release forms." The girl pointed at a tall table with client services staff speedily typing away.

"If your client paid, they will be able to print it out. If not, ask your client *kindly* what form of payment they would like to pay with; if it's cash under eighty thousand Hong Kong dollars or credit card, then go to the cashiers at that station." She pointed to another set of tables with other staff pushing each other out of their way. "Remember to secure a room at the gallery so you can show your client what they bought. If no rooms are available, which is highly likely cuz there's only three rooms available, god bless the interior designer, then you've got to see if your client is OK with you releasing the lot in the sofa area."

"Thank you so much! I'm Mad by the way, from the jewelry department. You are?"

"I'm Susan from the Chinese works of art department. Don't worry, you'll get the hang of it. Sometimes offering the client a coffee first works wonders. Oh! And Ophelia; she's in charge of the whole operation here, so don't get on her bad side; you'll see what I mean. Good luck!"

Why do people always say good luck over here?

Eventually, Mad made it to the front of the line to have client services print out the release forms. The girl was flustered and at the brink of tears. She typed quickly, pulled up the account information, and informed Mad that her clients had not paid yet.

Damn it!

Mad turned and looked over at the gallery to see if there were any rooms available so she could ask the clients politely, and in private, to pay. Unfortunately, there were none, and that meant Mad would have to kindly offer them the sofa area and ask in full public view.

Mad walked towards the door separating the chaotic gallery area from the Zen-like lobby. All the clients looked at her while the door closed behind. She scanned the room, trying to pinpoint anyone who looked like jewelry clients, but succumbed to calling the clients' name, like at a doctor's office, instead.

"Mr. and Mrs. Gunawan?"

An impeccably dressed couple stepped forward. The husband wore a white tailored suit with purple pinstripes, while his wife wore a purple minidress. She had full-on makeup and freshly coiffured hair. The unmistakeable purple crocodile Birkin and 10-carat diamond ear studs she was wearing all screamed out money and privilege.

"Yes! Finally!" they replied with haughtiness.

"Mr. and Mrs. Gunawan, sorry for your wait. There's an incredible line for the gallery rooms; would you mind taking a look at your purchased lot at the sofas over there?"

Both shifted their heads over to the sofa area next to the elevators. Their tense facial reactions told Mad she would regret what she just said.

Mr. Gunawan spoke first. "How can we just look at the brooch over there? Where is your security? What kind of service is this? Where is your boss?"

Then he spoke to his wife. "Love, I tell you, you can't just walk in here and expect service. Didn't I tell you to call so-and-so first? They think we are no one!"

Then he faced Mad again. "Is your boss here? Is Doreen here? I want to speak to her now!"

Mad quickly walked over to the lobby front desk and called the Boss.

"Mad, I have no idea who they are. It's such a small lot—so cheap! They must be Doreen's clients. Call Doreen and have her deal with it." The Boss hung up on Mad.

Mad quickly called Doreen and explained the situation.

Within a few seconds, Doreen ran down the stairs to the gallery. The clicking and clacking of her high heels on the marble floor announced her entrance before her frizzled hair and fluorescent designer clothing did.

"Mr. and Mrs. Gunawan. I'm so sorry for the inconvenience. The rooms are all occupied, indeed, but no worries; I called over a security guard, so we can admire what you bought at the sofas. Please come with me. Would you like a coffee?" Doreen wooed.

The couple looked very pleased to see Doreen and softened their scowling.

"Yes, coffee, please," Mrs. Gunawan replied.

Without a word, Doreen took Mad's tray and gestured for her to get the coffee.

Mad hurried over to the pop-up café at the side of the lobby and ordered for the clients. While waiting for the coffee, Mad could hear Doreen praise the clients' taste for buying the diamond brooch. How she had numerous clients bidding on the brooch, and they were "oh so lucky to get it." Mad was sure she had not seen Doreen in the auction room at all.

But from Mrs. Gunawan's giggling, it seemed they were pleased with the flattery Doreen showered upon them. Mad approached with the freshly brewed coffee. Again, without saying a word, Doreen handed Mad a black American Express card and dismissed her with a brush of her hand.

It was Mad's cue to handle the clients' payment. She went to the gallery and lined up at the cashiers to pay for the lot, then the front desk to print out the release papers, then back to Doreen and the clients. By then, they were gleefully retelling their most recent travel experience, and Doreen was laughing boisterously at everything they said. Mr. and Mrs. Gunawan didn't even give another glance to Mad as they walked out of Minos with their diamond brooch. The elevator door closed, and Doreen's smile dissipated as well. "Next time *my* clients are here, you better call me first," Doreen said sternly. She turned and left with the clicking and clacking of her shoes echoing throughout the room.

For real?

"Hey, she's like that. Don't feel too bad about it."

Mad turned around to see who was talking to her.

"I'm Henry from Watches," a Harry Potter doppelganger said. "Don't worry about Doreen. She doesn't have too many clients, so she's very territorial. She's going to lose her job soon if she doesn't perform." He wore a classic light blue suit, white shirt, and navy-blue tie. His round black-rim glasses made him look younger than his age and readily approachable.

"Thanks, Henry. I'm Mad from the jewelry department. I'm still trying to learn the ropes of this whole lot-release process."

"Well, I'm sorry to say, but this is the shittiest job ever. We juniors have to stick together, though, and help each other. So, if you have any questions, just ask me."

"Thank you, Henry!" Mad said, reassured already.

Mad headed back up to her department, expecting to have some time to look over the consignment terms and conditions. If Veronica wasn't going to help her, she would find out herself. The phone kept ringing off the hook, though; all the calls were from the front desk informing them of a client arriving to obtain their purchased lot. Considering the stressfulness and Minos's surprisingly inept handling of the whole release process, it was no wonder every time a client came, Mad, the new girl, was called to release the lot.

If Mad was lucky, the client had paid, and she only needed to line up for the release papers. The rooms were usually occupied, so Mad learned quickly that the best way to *get* a gallery room was simply to *take* it. Forget about all the pleasantries and signing-up procedures. If you had a client in the room, no one would dare ask you to leave. When no rooms were available to take, Mad simply used the coffee-and-security-guard trick. That seemed to pacify the clients enough for them not to make a scene in public. As rich as most of the clients were, most of them still loved a freebie. If they wanted more jewelry pouches or boxes, Mad gave them extra. As long as they were happy, Mad was happy.

The doors to the gallery finally closed at 6:00 p.m. Mad slumped down on the sofas with Susan and Henry, relieved the day was over. Mad's feet were swollen and in pain; she couldn't stuff her feet into her high heels anymore. Normally she wouldn't have, but she just couldn't stand it—Mad took off her shoes and heard a laugh beside her.

"Good idea," said a boy. He looked so young, as if he had just graduated from college. He wore a white shirt, black pants, and a pink Jim Thompson silk tie with a pattern of little elephants.

"I'm Liam, from the Chinese paintings department."

"I'm Mad, from the jewelry department. Long day for you too?"

"Oh my god! This is just the beginning!" Liam dramatically exclaimed.

"Yes, we have a few hundred lots to go," Susan added. "Let's not forget we have to return the unsold lots to the owners as well."

Mad hadn't thought about that before, but she was too tired to respond.

Henry jumped up from the sofa. "Guys, we can do it. As lowly as this job may seem, we *are* meeting clients, and sooner or later clients will start recognizing us. We have to do this anyways, so let's make the most out of it. Stick together and help one another. It'll make all our lives easier, yah?"

Mad smiled as she realized, through all of this, she was actually making some new and perhaps trustworthy friends.

The moment was promptly interrupted by Ophelia.

"Get back to your departments! What is it here? An episode from *Friends*?" Ophelia bellowed.

They jumped up and rushed to their respective departments. Indeed, tomorrow was another day, and Mad would be more prepared than ever, in flats.

It was up and down the stairs and running around the company for the next few days. Despite the circumstances, Mad was glad she met her new comrades. They were all busy releasing items to their prospective buyers or returning lots to the vendors, but it was nice to get a wink or a smile along the hallway. Way better than the solemn, serious faces in the office, which for some reason Mad was getting more of.

This is all happening because of the compliment the Boss gave me the other day.

Mad wasn't 100 percent sure, but she most certainly didn't have the time to confront the girls, nor did she want to.

I'm here to do my job and prove I'm an asset to the team. One day they will see me as that.

Ophelia turned out to be Mad's best ally over the coming days. With her tweed skirts and cardigans, she looked more like an old school librarian than a corporate head of something. Nonetheless, she knew everything that was going on in the company. Essentially, she made sure that all operations ran smoothly at the front line. From the release forms to payment to the gallery rooms. She handled the clients, the coffee, the cleanliness of the whole area. But more importantly, she knew all the clients, and all the clients recognized her. She remembered if the client wanted coffee or tea and even how many sugar cubes the client wanted. She had been in the company for ages; no one could remember exactly how long. But everyone knew that she had seen it all, and if there were any questions about anything, a client, a process, a person, Ophelia was the one to approach—if she liked you, that was. If not, she could make your life hell. If for some reason your release form was unprintable or the cashier could not find your client's payment in the system, even though your client had paid weeks ago, it was most probably because you had pissed Ophelia off.

Mad had been careful in her interactions with Ophelia but always managed a smile whenever she saw her. So far, all her releases were printed correctly, payments were shown on the system, and gallery rooms were made available to Mad magically if Ophelia knew beforehand that the client was predictably troublesome.

Lunch runs were not as awkward anymore. Mad just ate lunch with her new friends at the beautifully appointed office terrace where strangely no one went for lunch. Perhaps it was the humidity, and others preferred to eat in the air-conditioning, but the million-dollar view was too enticing for the quartet. Situated on the twenty-fifth floor of an illustrious building in Central, the terrace faced the quintessential postcard snapshot of the CBD and the Kowloon waterfront separated by the Victoria Harbour and its bustling nautical traffic. Directly on the right was the rooftop restaurant and bar Sevva, where high society lunched and bankers went for happy hour. On the left was a curious-looking penthouse with an outdoor pool that no one ever saw used. Having lunch at the terrace, Mad actually found out more about Minos than she would have if she stayed in her department.

Within a week of sharing their daily lunches, Mad already felt comfortable enough to ask her friends questions about the job.

"I tried to ask Veronica about consignments, but she told me not to think about it. I have to get consignments, though, or I will never become a senior specialist. Where do I learn about the pricing and terms and conditions?"

Liam looked at Mad like she was from outer space. "Honey, of course they wouldn't tell you how to get consignments; you're competition!"

"Remember, after that little comment from the Boss, you're public enemy number one," Susan declared. "You can sell lots already; they don't want you to bring in consignments too."

Susan and Liam were a wealth of information. They both joined the Minos master's program right after they graduated from college. After the program, they joined the company officially and hadn't left. Nor did they aspire to; as Liam once mentioned, "Why would I want to leave the most prestigious auction house in the world?"

Unlike them, it had taken Mad a while to get where she was now. As a little girl, Mad's parents and she would visit jewelry shops and look at all the scintillating pieces on display. Mad's parents weren't rich, but they were cultured enough to know how to admire these fine pieces and were adamant that their daughter know everything about them as well. Her father always told her that "A true lady knows her gemstones" and "never waits for a man to purchase one for her." It was along this train of thought that pivoted Mad to the Gemological Institute of America (GIA) school after she finished college, where she eventually obtained her Graduate Gemologist degree and entered the jewelry industry. She had worked her way up as an administrator to specialist trainee, then to a junior specialist.

With their limited knowledge, her parents always saw Minos as the epitome of auction houses. Mad knew they longed for her to work there, and that had become her goal.

"Don't worry, the terms and conditions are universal, it's all printed out," Henry said and pulled out a sheet of paper.

"You keep it with you?" Susan asked disbelievingly.

"Of course. What if I meet someone who wants to consign while I'm releasing a lot?"

Unlike Susan and Liam, Henry was as ambitious as Mad. Henry had had to work his way up from multiple auction houses before landing the job at Minos. He was a watch aficionado and had been interning at watch workshops ever since adolescence. Mad could already tell that Henry was as determined to rise up the corporate ladder as she was.

He looked down at the sheet. "So, for jewelry, here are the vendor commission rates. As usual, the more you consign in value, the lower your rate."

Mad looked at the paper and scanned the different vendors' commissions, determined by how much the client sold. The higher the amount, the lower the commission. Also, if the client was a trade client, the commission was lower than a private client.

"Other than that, there is the usual insurance charge and a marketing fee depending on how many pages your item occupies in the catalogue." Henry continued. "In other words, it depends on how important your consignment is. You know, all of these fees could be exempted, it depends on how much the Boss wants the consignment," Henry laughed.

"This is great! Thank you, Henry!"

"The only thing you need to learn is how to appraise the consignments," Susan remarked. "There's a database with all the lots that were put into auction, with estimates and the prices sold for. I think you should start there."

"But remember, don't let the girls see you doing it," Liam warned. "Who knows if they will sabotage you or not."

That was just the direction Mad needed. That day, Mad waited for everyone to leave the office before she acted. The boys left first, something about dinner with a client. The girls left right after they saw the Boss leave.

"Bye, Veronica; bye, Lisa; bye, Florence! See you tomorrow!" Mad said to them as the trio walked out the door. Ignoring Mad, they kept chatting and were gone.

She looked down at her neat pile of books and notepad on the left-hand corner of her desk and waited for the door to close tight.

Beep. The door closed, and the security lock secured.

Mad took a deep breath. Inhale and exhale. Then she quickly straightened up and grabbed her mouse to search for the database on her desktop.

It was easy. Just a few clicks and she found it! Lo and behold, every single lot that was sold in the history of Minos was in there. Every lot, their descriptions, estimates, and hammer prices.

Click. Click. Click. Click. Click.

Damn it! The information is not downloadable!

Mad closed her eyes and thought about what she could do. It took a few minutes, but she came up with a plan.

I'm going to have to manually input the data on an Excel spreadsheet. All I have to do is place them in categories where I could easily filter and find the corresponding estimates and hammer prices.

Mad decided she only wanted all the lots that had colored diamonds, colored stones, and natural pearls sold in the last five years from each of the sale centres of Hong Kong, Geneva, Paris, London, and New York. She didn't need lots with colorless diamonds since she could just look at the Rapaport Price List. She would input the data within categories of origin, color saturation, size/weight, clarity, shape, and treatment.

With this database, Mad could just make a few clicks, pull out past estimates and hammer prices, and be able to appraise any jewelry piece instantly and confidently. Mad knew at the moment she might not be able to automatically spit out recommended estimates to clients who wanted to consign, but at least she had this ultimate database to help her, and this would be her competitive edge over the others.

Approximately three hundred lots per sale. Two thirds of each sale with the lots I need. Two sales per sale centre each year. Five years. That means . . . about ten thousand lots to input. Let's get started!

Determined as ever, Mad typed away. Each day after everyone left the office, Mad stayed behind dutifully and worked on her database.

In the daytime, when Mad wasn't releasing the lots, she observed what the others did and, most importantly, observed how the Boss scored a consignment. It was still early in the season, but due to the success of the last auction, quite a few clients had shown up at the office with jewelry to consign. Whenever there was a chance, Mad would walk past or pretend to file papers in front of her office. She wanted to listen and grasp all that she could learn from the Boss—and perhaps substantiate what had been bothering her since the auction.

Are they fixing prices?

From what Mad could grasp, whenever there was a client, he or she would meet the gatekeepers, Ronald and Louis, first. They made sure the jewelry was acceptable before allowing the client to see the Boss. The Boss decided if the jewelry piece made it into the upcoming auction or not. Contrary to each owner's belief, most jewelry was not that sellable. It took at least half a year to curate a sale, which was why there were only two auctions per sale centre each year. It was difficult for Mad to learn anything, though, as most of these meetings happened behind closed doors. Mad had to find out more through her friends at the terrace.

"What do you think Ronald and Louis say to the clients to reject their jewelry? They can't simply say it's worthless; that would infuriate them," Mad asked during one of their lunch sessions.

"It's easy," Liam replied. "The most important thing is to let the client know how magnificent their jewelry is but give them such a low estimate that they wouldn't consider consigning."

"Or," Susan added, "just tell them you don't have clients for the piece, and you would hate to have them waste money on marketing and insurance charges."

"I've heard that if you suspect something is wrong with the gemstone, like it's fake, you could ask them to go to a laboratory to get a certificate first," Henry said. "Better to let the labs tell them than you. I've seen meltdowns in the gallery before, and it's not pretty!"

"Oh, and you can always suggest putting the piece in the online sale, then that team can deal with it!" Liam snickered.

"What if the jewelry is nice? What do you think the Boss says to get the consignment?" Mad questioned.

"You do know the Boss has a reputation," Susan said matter-of-factly. "She's known to have quite a few wealthy clients, so it's really not hard for her to persuade—I mean tell someone to give her a consignment."

Liam laughed. "That's right! Who wouldn't want to consign at Minos? You get the best chance of selling and for a high amount here. If not at Minos, I don't know where else."

"That's true. We were trying to sell this jadeite figurine, and no one bought it. But the next season, the client put it in the Minos sale, and of course, it sold." Mad relayed the experience.

"I know what you mean," Henry said with a nod. "But to answer your question, I'm sure there are occasions when a few auction houses are bidding for the same consignments. In that case, I would think the Boss would entice them with other terms."

"Terms?" Mad asked.

"It would have to be exceptionally magnificent, though," Susan said, widening her eyes.

"For sure!" Liam added.

"Yes." Henry continued. "If the Boss really wanted it for her sale, then she would offer more lenient terms and conditions. Such as exempting the marketing and insurance charge, or only charging when a certain price was met. She might *even* offer a guarantee for the item. It all depends on how the deal is negotiated."

"Oh! Don't forget IC!" Susan reminded them.

"I've heard that a client actually got as much as one million US dollars as an introductory commission," Liam exclaimed. "Minos didn't mind since the jewel generated quite a lot of press and in the end helped the company win market share. It didn't matter if they made money or not."

"That's incredible!" Mad gasped. "So, all the client needed to do was introduce someone?"

"Yup," Liam said plainly.

Mad gazed at the rooftop pool on the next building as she composed her thoughts. It seemed like there were numerous ways to get a consignment, and what one really needed was a chance. The only thing you could do was just prepare for it. Deep in thought, Mad stared at a person cleaning the pool.

Henry looked over as well. "Why do they keep cleaning that pool when no one ever swims in it?"

"I know," Mad said. "Maybe just in case the owner does one day want to take a dip."

♦   ♦   ♦

As the days went by, Mad managed to observe the team even more diligently. The Boss was always typing away in her office. The girls were either surfing the Internet or on their phones. Louis worked quietly at his cubicle. But Ronald was a spectacle. He constantly fidgeted in the tight three-piece suits that he wore every day. He twitched his face when he put on his heavily framed vanity glasses. All telltale signs of some confidence issues. But what really made Mad suspicious was how Ronald circled daily outside the Boss's office. He was the first to close her door when some conversation came up and *he* didn't want others to listen too. Not only that, he circled around each one's desk occasionally, just to check if anyone "needed help." Mad couldn't help but ask about him at the terrace.

"Do you guys know what the deal is with Ronald?" Mad asked. "He seems pretty insecure to me."

"He has an Ivy League education," Henry disclosed. "Plus, he's deemed to be the next 'the Boss.' He's being groomed!"

"He *is* very insecure. Have you heard him speak? He can't even decide to stick with an American or Chinese accent. You're not his target yet, but when it seems like you could threaten him, then he'll start stalking you for sure," Susan confirmed.

"He's actually quite well known for that. Well, when you don't have clients, as he doesn't, then you should worry."

"What do you mean he doesn't have clients?" Mad asked. "He's got so many telephone bids. Plus, he graduated from Harvard! What does he have to be insecure about?"

"He got a scholarship to Harvard. He didn't get in because he knew someone. In this business, it's who you know that matters, not how well you score on a test," Susan said.

"You think he has private clients? His bids are mostly from dealers, and dealers bid with anyone. He doesn't have the family background nor the charm. Of course, he acts so anal," Liam agreed.

Mad understood now more than ever that having private clients was the key to rising up the ranks at Minos. That's why Ronald had such a huge chip on his shoulder; he was not part of the exclusive club, and no matter how hard he worked, he never would be.

Henry looked at Mad. "Hey, it's not all about being in the club or not, OK? I believe if you work hard, you can make it too."

Mad smiled back at Henry and his reassuring words.

"Unless you're as anal and charmless as Ronald!" Liam squealed with glee.

They erupted in laughter; even the pool boy at the building next door looked over.

As much as Mad wanted to stay within the department to observe more, she needed a breather occasionally. Sometimes Mad just wanted to finish her work during lunchtime, but the girls would circle around the table in the back of the room and gossip about other people while eating. So-and-so was allegedly sleeping with a watch client, or so-and-so was sleeping with the head of the contemporary arts department, hence her recent promotion. They gave nicknames to every client and every colleague in the company and giggled at others' misfortunes.

"Oh, did you hear someone crying in the toilets?" Florence asked.

"Who's crying in there?" Lisa pondered.

"Is it Lola from the front desk? Did someone finally tell her to take a break from her makeup?" Veronica blurted out. "No matter how much she uses, she'll still look like crap!" They howled together.

Snickering, Florence corrected Veronica. "No, no, no. It sounded like Germaine from the Chinese works of art department. I heard a few days ago that her fiancé broke off their engagement!"

"Really!" Lisa cried sceptically.

"That's not surprising. Everyone knows the department has bad feng shui," Veronica blurted out. "Only spinsters work there!" She burst out laughing again with the girls.

Mad had had enough of the constant cackling. She decided to take a walk and catch a breath of fresh air.

I thought high school was over. Some people just never grow out of it.

At the door, Mad bumped into Henry. "Hey, Mad, did you have lunch yet?"

"Why? What's up?"

"I'm so happy; I just got my first big consignment for the coming sale! It's a Rolex Rainbow! Come let me buy you lunch!"

"Gosh, Henry! Congratulations. I'm not hungry, but let's walk together. Tell me more about how you found it!" Mad followed Henry down the hallway and listened intently to him.

"I was having dinner with a friend last night and was just talking about how great our last auction was and how I was so happy working at Minos and how proud I was. All of a sudden, this lady from the next table goes 'Excuse me, dear, I didn't want to eavesdrop, but the way you talked about your job really put a smile on my face, and I couldn't stop listening to what you had to say.'"

"Wow, she actually said that to you?"

"Yes! She must have been in her late forties, but she looked really fit and well kept. Red lipstick, Kelly bag . . ."

"She must be a tai tai."

They walked over the cross bridge to the building next door. The most convenient thing about working in the CBD was most certainly the indoor air-conditioned bridges connecting building to building. They took a golden-colored elevator up to the top floor and entered Sevva.

"Table for two, please," Henry said to the hostess before continuing. "Then she asked for my business card and said she wanted me to look at something she had."

"The Rolex Rainbow!" Mad said wide-eyed as they sat down at their table.

"Yes! This morning, she messaged me about it! You know, the one that has a colored-sapphire rainbow bezel and is so hard to find because it takes Rolex such a long time to sort all the stones and match all the colors. Her Rolex has a full diamond dial too!"

"No way!"

"I gave her an estimate from our last sale and told her what it could potentially sell for, and she actually brought me the watch an hour ago, and we just signed the contract!"

"That's the watch that had a record number of bidders, and the bidding took ten minutes! And in the end the successful buyer in the room just kept his hand up the whole time and finally won?"

"That's right!"

"Congratulations! Good job, you!" Mad said with elation, giving Henry a high five.

As they settled down, Mad finally looked at her surroundings. This was her first time stepping into the restaurant. She had only seen it from outside. A mixture of plush pink- and coral-colored chairs flanked pristine white-tableclothed tops. The pale pink walls were brightened by a vast number of artworks. The lush grey carpeting balanced the opulent crystal chandeliers illuminating the room. The floor-to-ceiling windows encircled the space, allowing the warm sunlight to pour in.

"Then if you don't mind, I'm not going to just have a coffee."

"Be my guest! I hear the caviar pasta is good here," Henry replied and raised his hand to order two.

Walking back to her office after lunch, Mad kept analysing in her head the details of how Henry secured the consignment. Honestly, there was no trick to getting a consignment. If the client trusted you, then the client would consign. Mad thought of how she could make people trust her. Lost in thought, she almost crashed into a person standing at the door.

"Sorry, are you OK?" he said.

"Yes, no worries!" Mad moved to the side. "Let me get the door for you. Are you here for the Boss?"

"Yes, thanks," he hesitantly said. He walked straight into the Boss's room and closed the door.

Mad walked back to her desk and had just started replying to her emails when she heard the noise in the Boss's office escalate.

"Must be another payment problem," Lisa conjectured.

Veronica added, "It's not like there's any other way to get payment from him. What is he going to do? Refuse payment for one of our top-selling lots?"

The girls burst out laughing, but abruptly stopped when the man barged out of the Boss's room. The girls quickly put their heads down and pretended they were typing or replying to messages on their phones. He looked defeated as he walked out of the office.

They started laughing again when the door closed. Mad rolled her eyes in disgust and looked out the window. The buyer obviously paid under another account that did not go through KYC, and that could be a telltale sign of money laundering. Auction houses had always provided a popular means to do so. As sensitive as the issue may be, Minos was a privately owned company; consequently, many transactions went through unnoticed and under the noses of auditors. The buyer's commission for these transactions was so large it was rare and highly unlikely Minos, or the Boss, would resist the payment.

As long as no one finds out.

Mad shook her head warily.

The door banged open suddenly. It was Ronald. He ran into the Boss's room, screaming, "Mrs. Tiovani is dead!"

"What! When?" The Boss looked shocked.

"This morning. Her gardener found her sleeping on her couch, but when it was noon and she still hadn't moved, he realized she was dead!"

Horrified, Mad looked at the commotion in the room. Yet, a grin slowly materialized on the Boss's face. Laughter erupted from the room. Mad was stunned.

Are they seriously laughing?

The Boss quickly put on her jacket and rushed over to grab her handbag. "Did you bring your appraisal records?" she asked Ronald.

"Yes, yes, I've got everything prepared!" As quick as the wind, they were both out the door.

Mad's eyes were as large as gumballs. She grabbed her phone and messaged Henry.

Mad:

> Someone just died and instead of condolences, the Boss and Ronald laughed! What is going on?

Henry:

> Who died?

Mad:

> Someone called Mrs. Tiovani

Henry:

> OMG! She's one of the biggest jewelry collectors in Hong Kong. She died?!

Mad:

Yes, that's what I heard Ronald say.
Apparently, she died on her couch. Her
gardener found her.

Henry:

Of course they are excited! She has no kids,
so all her jewelry is up for grabs now! They
must get there before D's does. Death is
the best thing that can happen nowadays

Mad:

Right . . .

Henry:

You guys just hit the jackpot. If they
manage to secure the mother lode, you
wouldn't need any more consignments for
the upcoming season. Think of all the press
and publicity

That was why the Boss and Ronald were so happy.
Mad wasn't sure if she should rejoice over the poor client's
fate.
Perhaps I should.
Mad was conflicted. Someone's woe was someone else's joy.
*Is that how we should be operating here? I'm not so sure
about that.*

❦ ❦ ❦

When Mad left the office that night, she still felt uneasy at what she'd witnessed. Instead of hopping on the MTR to return home, she decided to take advantage of the cooling weather and walk.

I might be able to clear my mind this way.

As Mad strolled, she looked up at the dazzling lights beaming out of the windows of the countless skyscrapers surrounding her. Hong Kong was not called a cement jungle for no reason. With an area of only about 1,100 square kilometres, you could easily get from one side to another within two hours of driving. Accommodating a population of approximately 7.5 million and hordes of tourists visiting each day, the only solution was the majestic high-rises seen all over town. As in any great city, it was easy to get lost in the numbers. However, Mad loved the hustle and bustle, and the efficiency of it all meant that anything could be achieved in a short amount of time. You just had to sow the seeds and wait for the flowers to bloom and flourish. If you worked hard, you would reap the rewards.

The moon was full, and a welcoming light breeze blew across Mad's face. She slowed her pace as others hurriedly walked past her. A couple holding hands sashayed in front of her and paused to laugh at a shared joke. Mad stopped behind them and waited for them to resume their pace. She was not in a hurry and was just trying to enjoy the moment. She gazed over at the other side of the street and noticed someone. The silhouette was so bold and authoritative, yet her movements strangely unfamiliar. It took Mad a minute, but she was certain it was the Boss.

The Boss, still in her office attire, was slumped over, helping a decrepit-looking man walk towards a white Mercedes parked on the side of the street. She gripped his arms and hands tightly as they inched steps closer to the car. The man wore grey pants, a striped shirt, and a newsboy cap on his head. The Boss wore a stern face that clearly indicated dissatisfaction. They reached the front passenger seat, but she was quickly reprimanded for the mistake.

"Not the front again!" the man barked angrily. "The back! Did you not hear me!"

Without saying a word, the Boss submissively diverted him to the back seat. Her head was bowing even lower than before. After carefully depositing him in the back and cautiously closing the door, she dashed to the driver's seat, slammed the door shut, and drove off.

As the car sped away, Mad looked on, dumbfounded. She had never seen the Boss as docile and powerless before—her whole persona crippled and castrated by this feeble man who obviously dominated her completely.

Who was he?

If anyone would know, it would be Liam. Mad decided to ask him tomorrow at the terrace.

▽ ▽ ▽

The next morning at work, Mad had not mentioned what she saw to a soul. She wanted to ask Liam face-to-face and see Susan's and Henry's reactions firsthand. In her mind, she couldn't stop replaying the scene over and over again. It intrigued her that an irate man could make the Boss cower helplessly.

When the clock struck 12:30 p.m., Mad rushed out of her office and ran to the terrace. By now, she was perpetually in flats, so she had no problem getting there quickly. She was so anxious to disclose her discovery that she didn't even bother buying her lunch first. Obviously, none of them had arrived yet. Mad succumbed to tapping her hand on the table while she awaited their arrival. To Mad's dismay, Henry and Susan showed up first.

"Where's Liam?" Mad asked in haste. "Is he coming?"

"He should be," Susan replied. "Where's your lunch?"

"Oh, I'll get it later. I have something to tell you guys."

"What is it?" Susan asked.

"It's something I saw last night. Someone. But I want to tell you all at once."

"You can have half of my sandwich," Henry offered.

"Thank you, Henry. I can't stomach anything at the moment, though. I have to let this out first."

Liam finally walked in with his posh take-out bag.

"Liam!" Mad shouted. "I've been waiting for you! I want to ask you something!"

"What happened?" an alarmed Liam said and rushed over to the table.

"Last night I was walking home, and I saw the Boss. She was helping this man, who looked sick and weak, into a car. The man screamed at her, and she just bit the bullet! I don't think the man is her father, though; he doesn't look that old. He—"

"That's her husband." Liam completed her sentence.

"What?" Mad exclaimed. "She's married?"

"That's the infamous husband no one has met before!" Henry said wide-eyed.

"Hard to believe, right?" Susan chimed. "That anyone would want to marry her."

"Or that anyone could stand her!" Henry asserted.

"Well, I just thought any woman of her stature and who worked such long hours would stereotypically be single," Mad explained.

"Rumour has it that he lost his job years ago"—Liam continued—"and the Boss has been the sole breadwinner of the household."

"Rumours?" Mad grappled with what she was hearing.

"They have a daughter, but she doesn't live in Hong Kong," Liam said. "From what I've heard, it doesn't seem like the family is that tight."

Silence fell over the table.

"He was barking orders at her," Mad mentioned.

"But come on, a woman like her would never get a divorce," Susan said. "Everyone would know she's single because she's a vicious bitch! Now, she would never want to fit into that cliché narrative."

"At sales week, I saw her looking at the president with those eyes," Mad relayed. "As if she really looked up to him. Adored him even."

"She definitely has a crush on him," Susan said. "Well, it's not hard to see why. President? Welfare? President? Welfare? I choose president too!"

"But she's not you," Mad said. "So, sadly, that's not a choice for her."

"That's not a choice she would give herself." Liam corrected her. "She's shackled to her own pride."

"The dilemma of a career woman," Henry said, nodding his head.

"No, it's the dilemma of a very self-conscious stone-cold career woman," said Liam, correcting him too.

Mad thought of what she saw last night. She also thought of the adoring eyes the Boss gave the president.

"She is human after all," Susan said.

CHAPTER FIVE

A flurry of weeks passed. Most of the buyers and vendors had picked up their lots, and Mad finally could relax a bit. The girls instinctively gave her some cataloguing to do. Not that Mad minded; she was an English literature major, so writing was never a problem for her. As a matter of fact, it did not take her long to write either. The record speed with which Mad completed the cataloguing fed the rumour mill, and that was when she was told to go into the Boss's room, door closed.

Unlike the rest of the department, the Boss's office was spartan and empty. The space was expansive, but the only furniture in the room was a desk and some chairs. On top of the desk was one small pile of books, a desktop computer, a telephone, writing tools, and a loupe. In comparison, all management-level offices she had been in had the basic couch-and-coffee-table setting. This office lacked that and other items such as accolades, framed photos, and artwork that would characterize or provide a story of the owner. It felt cold and uninviting.

"How are you liking Minos so far?" the Boss asked pleasantly.

Surprised that the Boss would even want to know, Mad replied, "It's great!"

"What do you think of the team?"

Everyone is a self-centred gossipmonger!

But Mad knew it was never wise to backstab anyone at work. It would backfire, especially when you were the newest member of the team.

"The team is very helpful. I've learnt so much from all of them."

Flashes of the Boss and her husband crossed her mind, as did the president and the Boss's adoring eyes. Mad cleared her throat, trying to focus on what was in front of her instead.

"That's good to hear. I'm glad that you are assimilating. Teamwork is very important here. I've had girls who couldn't work with the team, and they had to be let go," the Boss said. "I've been hearing such good things about you. You had no problems at all releasing the lots to the buyers and vendors, getting payment from your buyer on time."

Mad had not realized Jackie had already paid for the lot. She had been so preoccupied that she had forgotten to contact her.

I need to give her a call.

"Now you're even helping the girls with cataloguing. I'm most impressed with your taking initiative. Keep up with the good work."

"Oh, thank you, I will!" Mad replied ecstatically. "Do let me know what else I can do to help the team. There's not too many lots to release to the clients, and cataloguing has been—"

"Oh yes, I'm glad you mentioned that," the Boss interjected. "I've been so busy lately with Tiovani, and I still have some written interviews to finish up. Could you please help me with those?"

"Oh, of course!" Mad spit out without knowing what she had just got herself into.

Interviews?

"Great! Thank you, Mad. I'll send over the emails. Just type a paragraph per question and send it back to me." The Boss returned her attention back to her computer screen.

"Oh, OK, sure, sure." Mad turned around and walked out, a little confused about her new assignment and a little bewildered at her hastened exit.

"Oh, and Mad?"

"Yes?"

"Keep this to yourself, and please smile when you walk out."

Mad obediently put on a smile, turned back around, and walked out the door. As she walked back to her desk, she could see the girls, Ronald, and Louis all looking at her from the corners of their eyes. They were obviously trying to decipher what had gone on in the room. Which, to be honest, Mad was trying to do too.

An hour later, she received several interview forwards from the Boss. They were either from different publications or from the PR department. One of the interviews was already partially filled in but was littered with grammar and spelling mistakes. The interviews were nowhere near finished. The Boss basically wrote a few incoherent sentences, put in a few records, and forwarded everything else to Mad.

This is a mess! What did I get myself into?

Mad was deep in writing mode when she received a ring from the front desk.

"You have lot 3292 to release."

What bad timing.

Mad scurried to the panic room to collect the lot and descended to the gallery, hoping that this wouldn't take that long. The client had already paid, and all she had to do was release the lot to her. All the commotion from after the sale had died down, so the gallery rooms were pretty empty.

It should be a breezy few minutes.

♦ ♦ ♦

Mad walked out to the lobby and saw a familiar face in a flowy floral designer dress, exuding an air of elegance and class.

"Jackie? What are you doing here?"

"Um, I'm here to see you," Jackie answered. "Did you get my message?"

"No. What is it about? Is everything OK?"

"Yes, of course."

"Then let me just release this lot, and then let's grab a coffee?" Mad looked down at the release papers. *Ms. Jacqueline*— that was when Mad realized that this was the lot her friend Jackie had bought to save Mad at the auction. She had come to pick it up.

"Silly me! I'm so sorry, Jackie! Let's go into the gallery room."

Bashfully, Mad led Jackie into a room around the corner. She slumped down on her seat and let out a long exhale.

Jackie examined her friend from top to bottom before saying, "I'm worried about you, Mad! I haven't seen you in ages, and you seem a bit drained."

"I'm so sorry, Jackie. I've been trying to learn the ropes and help the team out. I've been meaning to contact you, but I keep on forgetting. I think this is just a learning curve, and by the next sale, I should be on autopilot. Thank you, thank you, *thank you* for helping me bid for this lot. Are you sure you want it?" Mad handed over the ruby ring and accompanying certificates.

"Oh, don't worry about it," Jackie replied without one look at the ring and certificates and tossed them in her handbag. "If your client wants it, I can sell it. If not, I need to get my mom a birthday present anyways. But what is most important is that you need to get out of this office and get a drink, for god's sake! I'm throwing a party at my house, so can you come?"

"Yes! Of course, tell me when and I'll be there. Thanks again, Jackie. I really don't know what I would do without you."

"Well, whether you like it or not, we're sisters for life since the first day we met at school!" Jackie laughed.

Mad joined in gladly. She needed a good laugh and was relieved to have Jackie in her life. How they became roommates in the first place was still a mystery to both. The school affirmed that the room assignment was strictly random. However, their backgrounds and lives were so different, it was hard not to wonder if they actually did it on purpose. Jackie was a jetsetter. She lived for charity balls, cocktails, and parties all around the world featured in countless *Tatler* magazines. Mad on the other hand did not even know what *Tatler* was until she met Jackie. "Anyhow, I also have something to consign to your next auction. Could you help me with that?"

"You want to consign something here? Are you sure?"

"Why? What's wrong?"

"Things don't feel right here." Mad moved her head closer to Jackie's and whispered, "I think I saw the Boss and Ronald pushing up the prices during the auction."

"That's not surprising," Jackie answered confidently. "I've heard rumours but from your competitors. D's to be exact. So, I don't know if it's lies or not. Do you have proof? Are you going to report them?"

"I don't have proof . . ." Mad's voice trailed.

"Are you going to stay at Minos, then?"

"At the moment, yes. I have to; it would look bad on my résumé if I left after such a short period."

"In that case, you're going to have to stay on board and just be careful. You're also going to need a consignment," Jackie, being the voice of reason, said reassuringly. Jackie had always been painstakingly straightforward and genuine. She would never hesitate to help any of her friends within her inner circle, which Mad was most certainly part of.

"Here."

Jackie took out a purple velvet box. She opened it and revealed the most beautiful pearls Mad had ever seen. About 8 to 10 mm each; they were all round and uniform. The dreamy lustre was the telltale sign that they were all-natural pearls.

The pearls Mad was looking at each had highly sought-after pink overtones. They were gorgeous. Mad believed she had just found a highlight lot.

"You want to sell this!"

"Why, yes, of course. They're a bit small for me," Jackie said matter-of-factly.

"But they're natural pearls! You can't find these anymore!"

"What's the use of this if I don't even wear them? Jewelry is for enjoying. In the words of Elizabeth Taylor, 'We are only temporary custodians of beauty.' Let someone else enjoy it."

"OK, if you insist. I'll go up and give you an estimate."

"OK," Jackie said and pulled out her phone to reply to her messages.

Mad ran up to the office and straight towards her computer. She quickly opened her database for natural pearls. She soon found a natural pearl necklace similar in size, lustre, and overtones. This was estimated at HK$4,000,000 to 6,000,000 and sold at HK$15,700,000. But this strand had the provenance from an Indian maharaja, so Mad decided to give Jackie's necklace an estimate of HK$3,000,000 to 5,000,000.

I hope Jackie will be OK with this estimate.

Mad returned to the gallery and told Jackie the estimate.

"Is it OK if we put this at three to five million? We sold one similar, with provenance, and it was priced at four to six million. But it made fifteen point seven mil in the end. I think with three to five million, we can attract a lot of buzz and bids, what do you think?"

"Sure, go ahead," Jackie said nonchalantly.

"Really? I can ask for some special shots to highlight your necklace as well. I think that would show how important it is, and maybe a special write-up?"

"Yah, go ahead. Don't worry about the special shots and write-ups. I'm sure it will sell."

"The commission is 5 percent, 1.5 percent insurance, 0.5 percent government tax, and finally about eight thousand Hong Kong dollars for the marketing fee. Is that OK with you too?"

"Yah, just go ahead. I'm sure it'll be covered." Jackie continued indifferently.

"Thanks, Jackie! Then I'll draft up the receipt and send you the contract for signing."

Mad quickly wrote the details on the receipt and double-checked to make sure all the details were correct. Jackie signed the document before they both headed out to the lift lobby.

"Remember my party, OK?"

"Yes, send me the details! I'll be there!"

After Mad sent Jackie off, she walked triumphantly back to the office and knocked on the Boss's door. Not presenting the Boss with the pearls first was a bold move on Mad's side, but she wanted to show the Boss that she knew what she was doing. Plus, Mad was sure the pearls would be a highlight lot.

"Hi, may I bother you for a minute?"

The Boss slowly looked up from her computer screen.

"What do you have there?" she asked with a stoic face.

"I've just taken this in from my fri—um, client. I think it might be something that would be great for our sale. The size, lustre, and overtones look like it should attract quite a lot of bids." Mad said this with as much confidence and professionalism as any specialist should have. She slowly put the tray containing the necklace on the Boss's desk.

The Boss took off her reading glasses and looked at the specimen. With a bemused look, she slowly touched it and held it up in the light.

Is she happy, or is she not happy?

Mad could not pinpoint the Boss's emotions.

"How much did you give your client?" the Boss finally asked.

"Three to five million Hong Kong dollars."

"Standard terms?"

"Yes."

The Boss finally looked up and smiled. "Ask Veronica to proceed with the contract and send it to SSEF for an updated natural pearl certificate."

"Could we also give it a few special shots and maybe I could add a write-up?" Mad asked.

"Why, of course, Mad," the Boss said. As she put her reading glasses back on, her smile faded, and she went back to staring at her computer screen. That was Mad's cue to leave.

Mad quickly took the tray and walked out of the room with a huge smile on her face. As Mad walked towards Veronica's desk, the girls quickly buried their heads in their cubicles, lest Mad see them eavesdropping.

Louis didn't even bother hiding his flabbergasted face as he stared at Mad. Mad had just brought in a consignment, her estimate was spot on, she secured special shots and a write-up for the highlight lot, and all of that for standard terms! It was clear from everyone's reaction that no one in the department had expected her to excel that quickly—especially when no one had taught her anything here.

Mad walked over to Veronica's desk and handed the tray to her.

Before she could even repeat what the Boss had said, Veronica looked at Mad with a huge smile on her face. "Let me work on the contract for you. I'll contact SSEF today and let them know that we have a natural pearl necklace for them to test," Veronica said zealously. "Look at this beauty; it's spectacular! Don't worry, let me process all the papers for you now."

Did I hear this right? Veronica actually smiled and complimented me.

Mad knew the tables were turning and grinned.

As she headed to her desk, Ronald abruptly burst into the office, dispelling the bizarreness in the room. He animatedly power walked into the Boss's room and swiftly closed the door. Outside the glass door, they could see Ronald saying something to the Boss, which in turn shifted the Boss's silhouette. Her head moved dramatically; angry noises escaped from the room. It looked like Ronald was using his hands to portray the signal to calm down before he was halted by a resounding smash. The Boss had slammed her hands on her desk. She threw her right hand up in the air, and more angry noises escaped the room.

Stunned, Mad watched the unfolding drama.

"I heard he lost a consignment to D's, a very important one," Veronica explained while her eyes were glued to the front of the room as well. "The client is from a very big family in Taiwan. He was so close to giving it to Ronald, but Ronald failed to secure payment for another lot that the client sold in the previous sale. He was not happy at all."

"What do you mean he failed to secure payment?"

"The buyer cancelled the lot."

"You can cancel the lot that you purchased?"

"Yah, if you're a very important buyer. Of course you can. In this case, the buyer just happened to be more important than the seller. Also, the buyer brought the jewel to Cartier, and Cartier said it was a fake. We had our doubts too, but Ronald insisted he'd authenticate it after the sale. So now Ronald must deal with the aftermath, which I'm guessing he didn't do well enough."

"Not only that!" Lisa jumped in. "The GIA results are in! The pair of 8.88-carat brilliant-cut diamond studs Ronald took in has fluorescence. I told the Boss this morning, and she was livid! Who's going to buy the diamonds now?"

"Seems like Ronald is not having a great start to the seas—" Florence couldn't finish her sentence. She was interrupted by a flustered Ronald swinging open the Boss's door, with a forced smile on his face.

"Veronica!" shrieked the Boss.

Veronica shot up from her seat and ran towards the Boss's room.

"Yes?" Veronica cried when she reached the door.

Everyone listened carefully to the Boss's orders.

"Cancel Ronald's ticket to the Geneva Magnificent Jewels sale. Ronald has decided he needs to go to Taiwan instead—for the sake of his career!"

Veronica diligently jotted down the instructions before asking bashfully, "May I ask, who will go to Geneva this time?" The yearning in Veronica's voice was evident.

The Boss looked at Veronica and said point-blank, "Mad will. She has a very important natural pearl necklace to show our clients there."

Mad's head snapped up.

Me? To Geneva? To an overseas sale already!

Mad's face glowed with exuberance. Getting to go to an overseas sale was a dream come true for any specialist. Usually it took years of experience before you were given a chance, but it only took her a few months. Not only that, this season, the sale in Geneva was even higher in value than the previous sale in Hong Kong. Mad felt like she'd just been promoted. The day had become *much* better than expected.

Everyone in the room stared at Mad. Louis's jaw practically fell off his face and hit the floor. Ronald disgruntledly rushed out of the office, hiding his fuming face.

Veronica walked towards Mad with a contrived smile.

She's really doing the best she can.

"Mad, could you give me all your passport details? Let me contact the travel agent and make the arrangements for you," Veronica said, as restrained as possible.

"Sure, thanks, Veronica." Mad was amazed at how controlled Veronica sounded, considering the tension on her face as she spoke.

CHAPTER SIX

It was hard to believe, but with a snap of the fingers, Mad's luck had changed drastically. Ever since that fateful day, the girls had been extremely friendly to Mad. The next few weeks, they offered to buy her lunches, volunteered to do all the administrative work, released lots, and repeatedly asked if she needed help with anything. At first Mad hesitated and refused their assistance. Their change in attitude towards her was blatantly obvious and made her genuinely uncomfortable. But their persistence eroded Mad's refusals, and she slowly took them up on their offers. Furthermore, she most certainly didn't want the Boss to think she wasn't a team player.

So, when the girls asked if they could go to Jackie's party, she couldn't say no.

"What are you doing this weekend, Mad?" Lisa asked.

"Oh, going to Jackie's house party. I haven't been hanging out much with her, and I promised I would show up."

"Wait, that's your friend Jackie who bought one of our top lots and consigned one of the top lots for our upcoming sale?" Florence asked.

"Um, yes, you could say that."

"Did you know her family is one of the largest developers in China? I heard they own a huge block up on the Peak and each family lives in their own house!" Florence added wide-eyed.

"I heard they hold the most epic parties! I've seen pictures of Mick Jagger partying there! Is that where you are going?" Lisa joined in.

"Yes, I am going to her house up on the Peak," Mad replied.

"Can I come too? I've always dreamt of marrying someone who lives on the Peak, and this might be the closest I'll ever be! Please!" Lisa asked. She was absolutely enthralled.

Mad tried hard not to roll her eyes.

What a pitiful dream.

"Can I come too?" Florence and Veronica chimed in together.

"Let me ask Jackie"—Mad yielded—"and get back to you."

Slowly, Mad messaged Jackie.

Mad:

Hey . . . is it OK if my colleagues come to your party tomorrow night? It's no big deal, just that they've never been to a house on the Peak before and it'll mean a lot to them . . .

Jackie:

Sure! The more the merrier!

"It's OK with Jackie," Mad said with a smile. "I'll send you guys her address. The party starts at five. I'll meet you guys there?"

"Thanks, Mad! You're the best!" said Veronica ecstatically.

"Thank you! Thank you! Oh! What should I wear?" asked Florence.

Lisa gave Mad a big hug.

Mad forced herself to reciprocate.

The next day, Mad arrived at Jackie's compound at around 5:30 p.m. Her taxi pulled up to the front gate and was stopped by a Gurkha guard. He inspected the car before checking if Mad's name was on the guest list. After authorizing her entry, the taxi drove down a slope to the fountain roundabout. Candles decorated the pathway, and twinkling lights danced on the foliage. Even the taxi driver voiced his awe with a big "Waaaaaaaaaaa."

It wasn't Mad's first time there, but every visit she was reminded of how beautiful the compound was. A doorman opened the taxi door for her, and she was automatically handed a glass of champagne. Mad walked down the brightly lit pathway leading to the lawn behind one of the houses. She messaged Veronica to see if they were there already.

Mad:

Hi! I'm at the house already. Are you guys here?

Veronica:

Yes! We are all here at the lawn.

Next to the pool!

Mad hurried over; she didn't want the girls to feel left out at the party. From afar, Mad could see a yellow blob. When she got closer, she realized it was Lisa. She was dressed in a sack that resembled a pineapple with feathers sticking out of it. It would have looked cute—on a child.

"Hey, Mad!" Lisa shouted as she held on to her finished champagne glass. "Do you like my dress? I bought it just for this party!"

"Hmmm," Mad faltered but couldn't say more.

Florence and Veronica appeared out of nowhere, and their outfits were equally if not more questionable. Florence was wearing a dress that looked like fishnets. You could clearly see her bikini inside. Veronica was wearing a transparent white dress that looked as if it were made from PVC. And you could also see her bikini inside.

Did they think this was a pool party?

"Oh, Mad! What a great party! I just saw Doug Woo!" Florence cried.

"Who?" Mad asked.

"Just the most eligible bachelor in Hong Kong right now!" Lisa chimed in excitedly. "Not only does he own Wheelock and all these other companies, but he's also ranked number one on the hottest bachelor list!"

"Where did you see him?" Veronica quickly asked while her head swivelled around trying to locate her prey.

"He's over there with this up-and-coming celebrity. You know the one in the latest Chinese drama? I don't remember his name, but he's so hot too!" Florence exclaimed.

"Where? Let's go and find them!" Veronica urged. Without any warning all three girls dispersed and left.

"Uh" was all Mad could utter. She was all alone.

"Don't you want to stalk the most eligible bachelor in Hong Kong too?"

Mad turned around and saw Mr. Lam facing her. With his baby-blue buttoned-down shirt tucked into his blue jeans, he looked sleek. He looked attractive too, as he stood before her holding a glass of whiskey.

As he walked over to Mad, she joked, "You mean the number-one-ranked hottest bachelor?"

"I didn't mean to eavesdrop, but I recognized the girls from Minos," Mr. Lam explained. "I just wanted to come over to say hi and let Veronica know that I will pick up my lots next week."

"Oh! You got something from the sale?"

"Something small, not too big. It will be a nice gift."

Mad quickly scanned his ring finger. No ring.

Girlfriend?

"Thank you for supporting us at the sale, Mr. Lam. And again, I'm so sorry about your shirt."

"Call me Steve. That's what the girls at Minos call me too."

"Steve," Mad repeated.

Awkward silence ensued.

Finally, Steve said, "I actually bought that ring you recommended."

Mad was surprised. "You did! Don't you think it's too small?"

"Well, someone told me otherwise . . ."

Mad looked at Steve's shy smile and smiled back.

"I'll come pick up the ring on Monday. Will you be there?" Steve asked timidly.

"Yes, of course."

"Is ten in the morning OK?"

"Oh! You want me to release it to you? Not the Boss?" Mad said, bewildered.

"Only if you don't mind," Steve faltered.

"Oh, I'm sorry, I can't Monday morning. I have an anti-money-laundering training. But I'm sure someone in the department can help you with it."

"How about later in the day? I have a meeting at eleven, but I could come at three? If that doesn't work out, I'm going to Shanghai for two nights, but I'll be back Thursday, so Thursday at four would work too."

All the money in the world and the only thing he doesn't have is time.

Steve added, "I'm sorry. It's family business. I've got limited choices."

"Sure, four on Thursday," Mad replied.

Steve's face lit up. "That's great! Thursday at four, it is!"

Mad smiled.

Steve took a step closer. "Perhaps you could tell me more about colored dia—"

"Mad!" Jackie barged in between them. "I've been looking everywhere for you! They told me you were here, but they didn't know where you went! My goodness!" She flatly added, "Hey, Steve."

"Hey, Jackie," Steve replied, but before he could start with the pleasantries, Jackie had already cut him off.

"Excuse us! I've got to catch up with this girl before anyone else takes her away from me!" Jackie forcibly tugged Mad away.

As Jackie ran off with Mad, Steve took a sip of his whiskey and said to himself, "I'll see you on Thursday."

◈ ◈ ◈

Jackie and Mad climbed up to a hidden balcony above the lawn area. Only a few people knew about its existence; it was strategically designed so that only the people sitting within could see what was going on below. Jackie plopped onto the cushions and caught her breath; her billowy summer midi dress rested slowly and perfectly as she sat.

"Phew! Finally!" Jackie exclaimed.

"Hey, Jackie, thanks again for inviting my colleagues to your party," Mad said, even though she regretted inviting the girls already.

"Oh, don't worry about it," Jackie replied. "Now tell me how it's going. How are they treating you? How about the Boss?" Jackie questioned.

Like an older sister, Jackie was always worried about her.

"I'm doing really well! I get to go to Geneva for the Magnificent Jewels sale at the end of next week!" Mad reported. "People in my department are talking to me—"

"What do you mean talking to you?" Jackie interrupted.

"Well, I think they saw me as competition after the auction, but now that I get to go to Geneva, it's like I'm in the Boss's good graces—it's better to support me rather than go against me."

"Mad, obviously they are jealous of you, and they're opportunists. You can't let them take advantage of you."

"I know," Mad sighed. "But I've got to work with them, so there's not much I can do now. You know it's always been my dream to work at Minos."

"And your parents'," Jackie added.

"Yes, that's true. But every company has its problems, and my goal is to work up the ladder and stay out of trouble."

"And your boss? How is she treating you?" Jackie repeated the question.

"She's a formidable woman, but she just gave me this opportunity to go to Geneva. It usually takes specialists years before they get this chance. I am quite grateful for that. Your natural pearls definitely helped with the decision. Thank you again! Regarding what I saw at the auction, I . . ."

Jackie straightened herself and sat closer to Mad. "OK, listen, Mad. There's a lot of talk about your boss. The way she conducts business is not clean," Jackie whispered. "Not only that, she's got a reputation for some shady business."

"You mean price fixing? You found evidence?" Mad eagerly asked.

"More," Jackie exclaimed. "Under-the-table money dealings! You know how easy it is for employees to sell directly to clients without going through Minos? It's just a matter of time before someone gets caught. So, just a heads-up, don't do anything you're not supposed to do. Do you even know why a position opened in the department? I heard the girl before you left because she was put in a difficult spot."

"Really?" Mad asked in disbelief.

What else are they up to?

Jackie continued. "And did you hear about the stone that had its color mysteriously altered after it was consigned to your boss? Allegedly, it was accidently overheated by the bench jeweler while he was mounting the stone! Frances says there was a huge cover-up because that bench jeweler is your boss's cousin! How unbelievable and unethical is that!"

Mad looked at Jackie with bewildered eyes. Jackie knew so many people and always had the most relevant information about everything. If she said it was true, it probably was. Mad sank down in her seat, deep in thought. There were so many opportunities opening for her in the department . . . But at the same time, Jackie's news was worrisome. The image of the Boss tapping Ronald under the table came back to her, as did the image of the Boss and her husband.

"Just make sure, whatever she tells you to do, you do it within company rules and regulations. Cover your ass before being a team player. It's not worth it."

To be certain Mad got her message, Jackie reiterated, "Be cautious, OK?"

Ding!

Jackie looked down at her phone and read a message. "Is there a Doreen or Gloria at Minos?"

Mad replied, "Yes, why?"

"They've been calling and messaging ever since the day of the auction. This is Gloria messaging me to go out to lunch with her again."

Mad was confused. "What? Why?"

Shouldn't they know that Jackie is my client?

"Well, this is what I'm telling you. There's plenty of sharks in your company. This happens everywhere, though."

"I never thought they would try to steal my client! They're so high up in the company! They have to resort to stealing too?"

"Don't worry, I'm going to block both of them from messaging me."

"Thanks, Jackie, you've always got my back," Mad said slowly, but clearly her mind was elsewhere. Working at Minos was like working in a war zone. Land mines were everywhere, but Mad knew she couldn't go back to a smaller auction house. That just wasn't an option at the moment.

"Well, I don't know what I would do without you either," Jackie said. "You know how fickle everyone in my social circle can be."

"And that makes you such a tough and strong person." Mad held up her champagne glass for a toast.

They both smiled but were quickly interrupted by the sound of a big splash at the pool. Jackie looked at her security cameras next to her seat.

"Your bloody colleagues just jumped into the pool," Jackie said bluntly.

Mad closed her eyes and exhaled. "You invited them."

◈   ◈   ◈

Thursday 4:00 p.m. sharp, Mad's phone rang.

"Hi, Mad, this is Ophelia. Mr. Lam is here to see you."

"Thanks, Ophelia, I'll come down now."

"My girls have escorted him to room three and are preparing his usual."

"Splendid, Ophelia!" Mad said admiringly. "What would happen to Minos without you?"

Ophelia chuckled. That was the first time Mad had heard her laugh. "Everyone is replaceable, my dear."

Mad grabbed the tray of jewelry she had previously prepared for Steve. He bought ten lots this sale, one of them being the 3.14-carat fancy vivid yellow diamond ring. She walked down the stairs into the gallery towards room three. She had already printed out the forms, so she was looking forward to a simple sign and release.

Mad knocked on the door and opened it, expecting to see Steve sitting down with his coffee. Instead he was pacing the room, talking on his cell phone.

"Yes, yes, the yield?"

Mad quietly sat down at the table.

Steve held up his index finger and mouthed, "One minute."

Mad waited patiently for him to finish. It was a full five minutes before he hung up the phone.

"I'm so sorry. There's a piece of land we are considering acquiring in Chengdu, and there's a lot of due-diligence work before we can act." He sat down across the table from Mad. "But enough about my boring life; how are you?"

"I'm good," Mad responded. "Here are your purchases; let's get started."

"Yes, of course. This gives me much more joy."

Mad pulled out the first piece of jewelry from a pouch. "Ten lots. Quite the shopper you are." It was a color change sapphire ring. Mad handed it over to Steve for inspection.

Steve gently took the ring from Mad. He had already pulled out his own loupe to look at the gemstone closely. "Well, it's more of my passion. Something I can decide on my own . . . without having to consult my family or a board."

Satisfied, Steve handed the ring back as Mad gave him the second lot to inspect.

"These are all your choices, right?" Mad asked.

Looking under the loupe, and with each turning of the facet, Steve answered, "Yes, my choices. My outlet. My escape."

"I know what you mean," Mad agreed. "I can look at them all day long. Each gem has its own story and—"

Steve's phone rang. "I'm so sorry, I have to get this. Hello. Yes. Talk."

Mad looked out the window as Steve paced around the room again. With an apologetic face, it was another good five minutes before he sat down again.

"I'm so sorry, I have to go. I don't need to check the rest; let me sign the papers."

"It's OK, don't worry about it." Mad handed Steve the forms and a pen to sign them.

As he was signing, he continued. "I've been so rude today; could I make it up to you? Are you free later for a coffee, maybe?"

"Oh, I'm heading to Geneva tonight. But really, don't worry about it."

"Geneva? For the sale?"

"Yes, to preview our lots and help out with the Geneva sale."

Steve finished signing and replied, "I see. Then I guess I will have to offer you a coffee next time."

Mad handed Steve an inconspicuous bag filled with his winning lots and led Steve out of the gallery. "Only a coffee?" Mad teased.

"I've been so bad mannered; I would be happy to offer dinner and redeem myself!" Steve exclaimed.

Mad laughed. "Next time."

Steve walked into the elevator. Before the door closed, he quickly added, "I'll take you up on that."

Mad smiled and walked back up to her office.

That's what they all say.

CHAPTER SEVEN

It took twenty hours for Mad to arrive at her hotel in Geneva. She was exhausted after being booked economy seats by Veronica.

I'm going to need to have a word with her. I'm pretty sure company policy indicates business-class seats for anything over six hours!

Dragging her luggage into the hotel Veronica booked her in, Mad couldn't help feeling uneasy. If Veronica was trying to sabotage her, this hotel was not going to be pleasant either. The hotel itself was eerily small and weary looking. Mad rang the bell at the front desk and waited. A tired-looking man appeared. It took him a while, but he finally found Mad's reservation and checked her in.

Sharks. I'll just have to make lemonade out of lemons.

Holding her room key and luggage, Mad rode the glass elevator up to her floor. There were bizarre life-sized wooden figures on the lobby of each floor. Thank goodness there was some light. If Mad hadn't been paying attention, she would have thought they were spookily real people. Mad reached the fifth floor and searched for her room. She walked to the end of the hallway and looked at the door front.

Room 5006.

Cautiously, Mad pressed the doorbell to make sure no one was in the room before she used her key card to open the door. The room was dark and grim. She slid her key card into the slot next to the door to turn on the lights and pulled open the curtains, letting the sun flood in. Jumping down on all fours, she checked under the bed and opened the closets to make sure no one was hiding under or within. Then she turned on the TV and automatically switched the channel to CNN. Now the room seemed less frightening.

Exhaling a sigh, Mad could now get ready for the previews. She quickly unpacked, showered, and meticulously applied makeup to perfection. Although she had travelled before for previews, this was her first time being in one as significant and large. The Geneva Magnificent Jewels sale was the highlight of the season. The most important and expensive jewels were placed in this sale and attracted the most distinguished clients as well as news coverage.

After she was all set, Mad took out her telephone and googled which hotel the preview was located at. It was just a block away.

Perhaps Veronica wasn't being spiteful after all?

Mad strolled to the preview hotel, absorbing the crisp, clean air and intensely blue skies. In the distance she could see the iconic snow-capped mountains of the Swiss landscape. Arriving at the grand hotel, she pushed through the revolving wooden doors into the stately marble lobby and was greeted immediately by a grandiose floral display.

I've arrived.

Following the signs to the Minos preview, Mad turned towards the foyer and was met by security checks and armed guards.

This is definitely more professional than our Hong Kong previews.

"Good morning, Madeleine."

Mad turned around and was stunned to see Javier. She was even more surprised he knew her name.

"That is your name, right? Did I get your name wrong?" Javier grinned.

Are those stars glittering around him?

Mad shook herself out of her paralysis.

"Hi, Javier! So sorry, I'm still a bit jet-lagged from the long flight," Mad managed to reply.

Javier reached in to give Mad a welcoming cheek-to-cheek kiss. Mad robotically followed and inhaled Javier's strong cologne. "We do it three times here," Javier said after the second kiss. Mad followed along, inhaling another big whiff of the spicy scent. It was intoxicating.

"You must have just got in. Here, let me help you with your bags." Javier chivalrously took her bags and walked Mad to her booth.

"How was your flight? Did you sleep well on the plane?" Javier asked.

"Not really, but it's OK. I'll be fine," Mad replied.

"Well, if you need coffee, just let me know; we can go out together to grab one," Javier said with a wink. "I know this great coffee place around the corner. Nothing like that Starbucks crap."

"Sure, maybe later this afternoon?" Mad suggested.

"Yes, you're going to be jet-lagged by then," Javier said, looking straight into Mad's eyes.

"Thank you," Mad said and gave Javier a very appreciative smile.

"You have such a sweet smile," he responded.

Flustered, Mad's heart skipped a beat. "I, um . . ."

They reached Mad's booth before she could embarrass herself further.

"Here's your booth. Your jewels have arrived, and John here from Security can help you open the locks." Javier pointed to a stoic man with a gun holstered on his belt.

He gave Mad a nod.

"Louise over here is your helper. She's been with us for a few seasons, so she can help you set up and get familiarized with the preview operations. But of course, if you have any questions or need anything, you can come find me," Javier said and showed his sparkly white teeth.

He turned around and left, a trail of his delicious cologne lingering in the air.

Mad looked back at Louise and shook her hand. "Hi! I'm Mad from the Hong Kong jewelry department. Thanks for helping out."

"Oh! No problem! I love helping your department out," Louise answered excitedly with a strong French accent. "You always get some amazing pieces, especially from Wallace Chan. Spectacular!"

"I'm afraid we only have one piece from him this time. The others are just single stones. The Boss wanted to showcase just a few top lots this time. We have a Kashmir sapphire, some Burmese rubies, Colombian emeralds, some smaller colored diamonds, and of course, natural pearls that she thought would be good for the Geneva market," Mad explained to Louise. She took out Jackie's natural pearl necklace to exhibit at the centre of the showcase.

Louise gasped. "This is amazing! Look at the lustre and overtones! Are these all natural?"

The certificate from SSEF had come back confirming all the pearls were natural. Louise's excitement reaffirmed how truly rare and beautiful the necklace was. After admiring the pearls, they set up the showcase as quickly as possible. The doors were to open at 10:00 a.m.; by 9:55 a.m. all jewels were in place. Louise was wiping the showcase while Mad placed a small glass of water in each case. The water kept the showcases from heating up from all the spotlights. They were ready.

Ding!

It was the Thailand representative.

> Hi Mad. Could you kindly look at a few lots for my client? Please kindly send me the condition reports, images worn and any other comments for these lots:
>
> 1401
> 1402
> 1403
> 1424
> 1426
> 1439
> 1454
> 1456
> 1458
> 1462
> 1463
> 1478

1480
1501

Thank you

The Boss had a talk with Mad before she left the office and told her specifically that her job was to showcase their Hong Kong jewels and get bids for their sale; everything else was secondary, including helping the representatives look at the Geneva jewels. Also, she had to follow the jewels to the dealers' tables and make sure they didn't throw around and damage the lot.

"Remember, sell our jewels first!" The Boss's words reverberated in Mad's head.

Mad knew of the competition between sale centres. That was why the Geneva team tried so hard to make sure they had a larger sale than Hong Kong did this time. Mad politely messaged the Thailand representative.

Mad:

I'll get back to you as soon as possible.

I'll just have to do it after hours tonight.

Louise asked, "Can I help you with something?"

"Ah, no, it's OK," Mad sighed. "I just have some Geneva jewels to look at for our Thai rep."

"Do you want to go take a look now? I can man the showcase for you," Louise offered.

"No, don't worry about it; I'll just do it later. Thank you."

Right on the dot at 10:00 a.m., Mad could hear clients rushing into the preview room. Most of them went straight to the Geneva jewels. This season, they had an incredible historical raja collection. It featured a spectacular array of jewels from the royal families of the Mughal dynasty. Most highly anticipated were pieces designed by European jewelry houses, such as Cartier, which gracefully combined the decorative qualities of the East and West. The front of the preview room was literally covered with diamonds the size of quail eggs, chunky colored-stone rings, countless natural pearl necklaces, bejeweled swords and daggers, feathered *sarpechs*, whimsical designer brooches, and shimmering objects of virtu. The concentration of extravagance in the cramped room and the accompanying enthusiasm was so overwhelming that hordes of clients had to be regulated to enter the showroom and, at times, given a polite berating to wait their turn.

The jewelry pieces beguiled the clients as they inspected and tried on the pieces. Ohs and aahs escaped their mouths as they feasted their eyes on the collection. The clients slowly trickled into the other showroom, which featured jewels from London, Paris, New York, and Hong Kong. Finally, clients arrived at Mad's showcase asking to look at and try on pieces. Mad had never seen such a concentration of impeccably dressed and polished clients in her life. Men were dressed in Sunday suits of endless shades of greys and browns while women were decked out in cashmere and furs. As these clients brushed past Mad's showcase, their pungent colognes and perfumes lingered. Mad's eyes feasted on these exotic peacocks surrounding her, but she was inevitably interrupted by a dealer. Dealers frequented the Geneva auctions, as plenty were headquartered in the city and had storefronts by Lake Geneva.

"I would like to look at these pieces at the dealers' room. Thanks, I'll be inside." The dealer passed Mad a piece of paper with lot numbers written on it. He went straight into the viewing room, where he could properly inspect the pieces with appropriate lighting and tools.

Since the jewels couldn't be left with the dealers alone, Mad assembled the pieces and brought them over herself. She waited patiently for him to finish examining them before she returned to her showcase.

♦ ♦ ♦

As the day went by, the rooms became more and more crowded. The dealers had to wait in line just to enter the viewing room. Mad rushed back and forth with the jewels; she was sweating bullets. She kept hearing her phone buzz, which made her even more anxious and stressed. They were all messages from different country representatives asking her to look at Geneva jewels for their clients.

"Mad, I can help you with the viewing tables," Louise offered as she saw how swamped Mad was.

"I wish you could too, Louise," Mad replied desperately. "But the Boss specifically said that either the pieces stay at the showcase or with me. Honestly, I'm exhausted!"

Louise handed Mad a much-needed bottle of water and some chocolates for energy. "Here, have some before you faint!"

After downing the whole bottle of water, Mad told Louise, "I've been getting messages from the reps, asking me to look at the Geneva lots and send them condition reports. I was thinking of getting it done after the viewing closes today."

"That won't work. There's a cocktail party tonight," Louise replied. "You won't be able to see the Geneva jewels."

"No! Really?" Mad's heart dropped.

"Are the requests urgent?"

"They seem like it."

"Let me see what I can do." Louise rushed out of the booth.

"Wai—" Mad could only manage to say before Louise disappeared into the crowd.

Great, now I've lost my helper, and I've got to stay put at my booth.

Mad tried to assemble another tray of jewels requested by a table of Indian dealers. But before she could finish, a mink-clad lady and her friends asked to see the Wallace Chan ring.

"What a beautiful piece!" the lady in mink exclaimed. "I love Wallace Chan's pieces. Do you know when he made this?"

"Madam, I'm afraid I don't know when it was made."

"Oh, what a wonderful piece." The lady continued speaking as her friends started taking pictures of her modelling the ring. *Then* each of them took turns trying on the ring *and* taking pictures of each other wearing it.

Oh my god! How much longer is this going to take? I need to show the dealers these jewels before they start yelling for me.

Slowly, Mad started sinking lower behind the booth; her knees and feet had started failing her.

"Mad?"

It was Javier with Louise.

Mad said, "Javier?"

"Louise tells me you might need a little help."

Like a knight in shining armour, Javier took Mad's hand and helped her up from her slump.

"Look, I know your boss doesn't like it when we touch her jewels, and we all know the Geneva sale is the least of her concerns," Javier said simply. "But we're a team at Minos, and I'm more than happy to help. So, why don't you let me know which of your Asian clients need condition reports and comments, and I'll email them from here. The sale is in a few days, and I'm afraid it might be too late if we give them the information right before the sale."

Mad looked into Javier's eyes, and as much as she didn't want to admit it, she realized she needed help. She pulled herself together and stood up straight.

Looking into Javier's eyes, she replied, "I agree with you, Javier. We need to send the clients condition reports and comments for these lots now. Qian Qian's clients are the following . . ."

Louise pulled out a piece of paper and handed Mad a pen.

Mad started writing down each representative's name and which lots their clients requested, as Javier watched and listened intently.

"Please also cc each of the representatives on the email as well," Mad finished.

Javier took the piece of paper and walked briskly out of the booth.

"Javier?" Mad said.

Javier turned around.

"Thank you."

"Señorita, it's my pleasure," Javier said with a wink.

The rest of the afternoon, Louise manned the booth while Mad went back and forth from the viewing tables. The crowd started to wane, and the girls were finally able to grab some food and, most importantly, go on a toilet break. Mad had been steadily receiving emails from Javier; even though she hadn't asked to be, she was dutifully cc'd on each email he sent out to the clients and representatives. Every single email was superbly written and beautifully descriptive: the pros exemplified, while the cons were only lightly touched upon. They each ended with an invitation to write him back, and he would respond "without any hesitation." Mad couldn't have done it better. She breathed out a sigh of relief after reading the last email. Louise hummed while she cleaned the showcase glass. It was the end of the first day.

"What a successful day. We got such a great response today and look, two bids! I'm sure your boss will be happy," Louise said.

"Thanks, Louise, for today," Mad said. "I'm glad you asked Javier for help."

"It's nothing! I didn't know if I was out of place, but I just couldn't see you suffer like that anymore. The Boss is notorious, but if she does blame you, you could just tell her it was all my fault."

"Don't worry about it. You made the right decision."

"And have we made any decisions for dinner tonight?" Javier strolled into their booth.

"I have to go find my boyfriend. I'll see you tomorrow, Mad," said Louise as she left with her handbag in tow.

"Thank you, Javier, for your help today," Mad quickly said. "I'm so sorry for causing you such trouble. You must have better things to do."

"Look, Mad, my job is to help the sale and, most importantly, our worldwide jewelry team. Stop feeling bad! I'm your guy, right? So, how about we go grab dinner?" Javier said with a glint in his eyes.

Mad felt tired and jet-lagged. Physically she wanted to go back to her hotel room, but mentally she wanted to go out with Javier.

Sensing Mad's hesitation, Javier said, "Come on, it'll be quick. Can I just see that beautiful smile of yours for a little while more? How about Japanese? It's just around the corner. I'll go grab my jacket and meet you in front." Javier turned around and went to retrieve his belongings.

Mad quickly put on her coat, took her bag, and rushed out to meet Javier.

◈ ◈ ◈

The Japanese restaurant was actually a few blocks away. They arrived at a generically decorated restaurant with pseudo-Japanese calligraphy and furniture. As the hostess led them to their table, they walked past a teppanyaki table. The chef earnestly performed tricks as he cooked the guest's meals.

Javier and Mad sat in a quiet corner at the end of the room. Looking at the menu, Javier asked Mad what she would like to eat.

"How about some tuna belly to celebrate the end of the first day?" he suggested.

"Tuna belly? I've only tried tuna before," Mad replied.

"What do you mean you've never had tuna belly sashimi before? That's the best part!" Javier uttered in disbelief. "Then you must try it tonight. Waiter!"

"No, no, no, don't worry about it!" Mad said bashfully.

"I insist!" Javier urged.

Mad was glad she'd gone out to dinner with Javier. As they ate, he charmed her and made her laugh. Mad had not laughed so hard since she joined Minos. They talked about current events, office gossip, and anything utterly silly. Such as how a certain colleague had been so obsessed with an auctioneer that he would mimic the way he dressed, talked, and moved. It was all fun and laughs until the day he showed up at work wearing the exact clothing and brand, down to the color of the socks. His behaviour became so bizarre that he had to be asked to go politely. "That's not even the most ludicrous thing I've heard recently!" Mad added. "Did you see the news about how one of the smaller auction houses hired an ex-CIA agent as the head of Security and—"

"Only to be arrested at JFK a few months ago for espionage," Javier replied matter-of-factly. "Yes, we all heard of that. The board demanded we run an updated background check on all our security personnel, even after HR assured them that such a mistake would never have happened in our company in the first place. I was stuck in endless meetings with people shouting at each other over this issue. It was a shit storm."

Mad looked at Javier with sympathy. They changed the subject to what they thought about the jewelry industry, such as the rise of Gemfields and the future prospects of Zambian emeralds in the auction market.

Javier is indeed as fun as he is intelligent.

"So, tell me, what do you think?" Javier asked eagerly as Mad tried her first tuna belly.

"Wow! It's really oily!" Mad exclaimed.

"Here, have some tea, it'll wash it down." Javier handed Mad a cup of tea.

As Mad took the cup, their fingers touched. Mad felt an electrical surge shoot through her body.

Mad quickly gulped down the tea. "So, what do you like doing in your free time?"

Javier was already reading his email. Mad looked at him, mesmerized by his handsome chiselled face and how serious he looked while attending to his emails. He finally looked up and replied, "Free time? I really don't have any! But I'm looking to settle down, start a family soon. All my friends have done so, and it seems like I'm the only one left. I love kids, just need to find the right girl; you know what I mean?"

And he wants to start a family too! And kids! He's perfect!

"What do you like doing?" Javier inquired.

"Oh, I like—"

Ding!

It was Mad's phone.

Ding!

It was Javier's phone.

Both looked at their phones. Mad saw an email with *Important* in the subject heading, from the president of Minos and written to the global jewelry department.

Mad quickly skimmed the email.

> ". . . Monsieur Allard has informed me that his jewelry record was incorrectly stated in the Prestige Hong Kong magazine interview . . . his record was much higher than . . . we never make mistakes at Minos . . . deeply embarrassed by this matter . . . make amends immediately . . . serious repercussions . . . warning letter . . . HR . . ."

It dawned on Mad that this was one of the interviews Mad wrote for the Boss, even though the Boss claimed credit for it. Before the Boss forwarded her the interview, she'd written a few numbers and told her specifically that there was no need to double-check *her* accuracy—which unfortunately in this case, was not accurate at all.

As the gravity of the email sank in, another email appeared. It was from the Boss. Mad skimmed the email quickly.

"I apologize for the mistake made by the new subordinate in my team . . . Madeleine is new to the team . . . will make sure she double-checks her work next time . . . not acceptable . . . this will never happen . . . will issue an apology . . . correction sent to Prestige magazine . . ."

Mad could not believe *this* email.

Did the Boss just throw me under the bus?

Sensing what just unfolded through Mad's appalled face, Javier took Mad's hand. "Don't worry about it."

"But she told me not to change the numbers . . . ," Mad replied, still looking down at the email.

"We all know how your boss operates, it's not fair, but she's your boss, so you just have to take it for the team," Javier said. He added, "Don't worry about it; it's really no big deal."

Take one for the team, Mad.

"You think so?" Mad looked wearily into Javier eyes.

Javier took his hand away. "Mad, you have to remember this. In this company, you can make as many mistakes as you want—be as crooked or shady as you want." Javier paused and took a sip of wine. "As long as you make money for the company, they will turn a blind eye."

Mad's spirit was dampened by the email, but Javier was still in good spirits. Mad tried to be as upbeat as possible and pretend nothing had happened throughout the rest of the dinner.

At the end of the night, Javier walked Mad back to her hotel. At the first crosswalk, Javier smoothly slid his hand down and held Mad's hand. Mad felt the electricity surge but resisted pulling her hand away. They walked along Lake Geneva and gazed at the swans swimming by. With the iconic Jet d'Eau in the background, it was the idyllic romantic backdrop. The air was chilly, but Mad was starting to feel uncomfortably hot. When they reached the lobby, Javier gently let go of her hand and kissed her lightly on the lips.

"I'll see you tomorrow!" Javier said as he turned around and left Mad standing alone.

Mad passed by the lively bar in the lobby and took the elevator back to her room. She opened the room door and sat on her bed; it was just 10:00 p.m. She turned on CNN. There'd been another shooting in Florida. There were people crying and hugging each other and an aerial view of people running out of the building. On and on the footage replayed. Finally, Mad jumped up; she couldn't stand this anymore. There were too many thoughts inside her head, and she needed to sort them out. She took her bag, left the room, and headed down to the hotel bar.

Plenty of people were seated at tables, talking or staring at the live band playing in the corner of the room. Mad shifted in between the rounded couch seats towards the glowing bar. She found an empty stool and sat herself down. The bartender appeared and in his thick French accent asked Mad what she wanted to drink. Mad looked up at the extensive selection of liquor bottles on the wall, but she couldn't decide.

Defeated, Mad finally said, "I'll just have a sauvignon blanc, please." The bartender nodded and left. Sitting alone at the bar was just what Mad needed. She wanted to think about the whole situation. The noise at the bar helped her drown out all the distractions and cleared her mind. She was angry at the Boss.

It wasn't the first time one of her seniors had screwed her over, but she just didn't think that the Boss would make such a mistake. And how she could so blatantly put the blame on her as if Mad was disposable?

Javier was right. It really didn't matter. As long as I have sales to show, I could make as many mistakes as I wanted, and no one would care. And Javier. What was that kiss about? Is that his friendly way of saying goodbye? Or is it more?

Mad had put her love life on hold for her career. She knew she had to be focused and disciplined to reach her goals. Time could not be wasted on frivolous relationships.

But what about now? Perhaps I could let go a bit . . .

"Hey, Mad."

Mad almost jumped out of her chair! It was Steve.

"Oh my goodness, Steve! You scared me! What are you doing here?"

"Oh! I'm sorry! I just wanted to say hi. I was walking past and saw you through the windows, sitting alone. Am I disturbing you?"

"Oh no, I'm just having a drink. I needed to clear my mind." Mad let out a big sigh.

Steve just stood there but finally said, "If you don't mind, may I join you?"

"Oh, sure, sure. Are you here alone too?" Mad replied.

Steve sat down on a stool right next to Mad's. It was so cramped their legs and arms touched each other.

"I was just meeting up with a few friends at Four Seasons, but I could have a drink here first."

Steve waved the bartender over and ordered, "Macallan on rocks."

Mad could feel Steve's warmth seeping through his shirt and pants. The silence was uncomfortable, but Steve didn't push her to tell him what happened. Finally, Mad just blurted it out.

"I just received an email reprimanding me for an interview I ghostwrote for the Boss. A record was incorrectly written, and she blamed me for it. She wrote an email to the whole company and said it was my mistake! I'm very upset—no, I'm furious!"

Steve looked over at Mad and her almost empty glass and signalled the bartender for one more order.

When her drink arrived, Steve eventually spoke. "You know, Mad, I'm a very busy man, tied to my family's business. Collecting jewels and gemstones is an outlet for me. Something I love doing and has nothing to do with my family business." Steve took a sip from his drink and continued. "I can tell you love jewelry as much as I do, and not because of the glitz and glamour of it all. It's because you actually appreciate it. So, I'm telling you this, you must be extra careful in your department. Whatever you're looking for at Minos, find it and leave. It's not a place for dwelling. Leave before you lose yourself and forget your values and morals."

Mad looked at Steve, dumbfounded. She hadn't expected him to say anything insubstantial, but she most certainly had not expected him to give her such raw, unfiltered advice.

Why would he tell me this?

Puzzled, Mad did not know what to say.

Steve stood up from his seat and signalled the bartender to give him the bill. He had to go, but before he did, he leaned in and kissed Mad gently on her cheeks. His warm lips brushed her face ever so softly.

He excused himself with a bye and walked swiftly out of the bar, leaving Mad even more confused than ever.

CHAPTER EIGHT

If Steve's words and baffling tenderness hadn't cast a dark cloud over Mad, the weather the next day most certainly did. It was grey, windy, and cold. Mad walked towards the preview still dazed over last night's events. Deep in her thoughts, she tripped over something on the ground but managed to catch her balance and avoided falling over. She looked at what she had tripped over and realized it was a girl huddled on the ground, picking up pieces of paper lying on the pavement. Mad quickly knelt and helped.

"I'm so sorry, are you OK?" the girl asked.

"Oh, don't worry, let me help you." Mad hobbled around and picked up several pieces of paper, while passersby ignored them. After collecting all the papers, the girls stood up, and Mad could finally have a better look at the unfortunate person.

She was gorgeous! She had the daintiest face but big doll-like eyes and the longest lashes Mad had ever seen. The lashes matched her dark hair perfectly. On cue, the wind blew her tousled hair. Mad couldn't help but stare.

"Thank you so much for helping me," the girl said.

"It's no problem," Mad replied, trying hard not to stare anymore. She finally walked away, back on track to the preview. The girl followed closely behind her until they both reached the hotel door.

"Are you heading to Minos too?" Mad questioned.

"Yes, I'm meeting my boss there. You?" the girl asked.

"I work here. I'm Madeleine from the Hong Kong jewelry department, but you can just call me Mad."

"Mad, I'm Fiona. Pleased to meet you," Fiona replied and held her hand out for a handshake.

How formal!

Mad automatically held her hand out as well before realizing a few men in tailored suits and earpieces were standing behind them. Suddenly, a tall young man in an impeccable suit walked up to them.

"This is Madeleine from Minos," Fiona said to the young man. "She was just helping me with the papers."

"Nice to meet you, Madeleine," the young man said and gave Mad a warm smile. Mad could finally see his face clearly. He was Middle Eastern, a young man in his early thirties, tall, handsome, and his suit exemplified wealth. His British accent indicated that he probably studied in the UK. What stood out the most were his eyes. They were warm and brown, and they looked kind.

"It was really no trouble. I couldn't—"

"Your Royal Highness!" It was the president of Minos himself barging through the hotel door.

"I was wondering where you were! Do come in from the cold! How was your trip from Qatar?"

"Please excuse us," the young man said as he smiled and was escorted by the president into the building. His entourage trailed behind with Fiona following faithfully as well.

The moment was quite surreal, and it seemed that Mad had just met royalty from the Middle East and his personal assistant. Mad knew a lot of Middle Eastern clients frequented Geneva, but she never thought she would meet one, let alone talk to one.

Only at Minos. What an experience to remember.

Mad walked briskly to her showcase and got ready for another long day of previews. She needed to concentrate on redeeming herself and proving that she belonged at Minos. Thankfully, she'd figured out a way to speed up the dealer viewing process. Instead of waiting for the dealers to inspect the jewels and calculate the prices, Mad barked out the significance of each piece, such as the carat weight, origin, treatment, and price per carat, so the dealers didn't have to do it themselves, and Mad could return to her showcase as quickly as possible.

Mad picked up her new strategy instantly, and without a hitch, she was able to cut down her time spent from dealer to dealer dramatically. By noon, a dealer looking at a rectangular-shaped emerald asked Mad, "Are these—"

"Eight point eight seven carats, Colombian, Muzo, no oil, SSEF and Gübelin certs!" barked Mad.

"What is the—"

"Sixty thousand per carat!" Mad replied, instinctively knowing that the dealer wanted to know the price per carat for the emerald.

When pearl dealers arrived at her showcase, she automatically showed them Jackie's necklace and the SSEF lab report to prove that all the pearls were natural.

Whenever there was time, Mad would run over to the Geneva preview showcases and quickly responded to the enquiries for their sale. She took pictures of the jewels being worn and messaged them directly to the representatives and clients with snapshots of the condition reports. This way was much more efficient than locating a computer to send emails. She knew she was on a roll today and was almost certain she sold Jackie's necklace when a dealer she showed the pearls to earlier in the morning came back to take a look at them again late in the afternoon—this time not at the dealers table, but directly at Mad's booth.

"Beautiful, isn't it?" Mad enticed him.

"It's one of a kind," Louise added.

"Hmmm," the dealer replied and continued examining each and every pearl.

Slowly, other dealers started surrounding the man, and one of them asked, "I thought you were going to bid on those new Paspaley natural pearls at D's? These are all old natural pearls, you know."

To which the dealer replied, "Age doesn't matter, as long as it's beautiful." All the other dealers started agreeing with him by nodding their heads in unison until one of the dealers blurted out, "Like women." And they all exploded into laughter.

"Would you like a telephone-bidding form for our sale?" Mad cut in.

The dealer didn't take his eyes off the pearls but smiled and replied, "You'll hear from my office soon."

After the dealer walked away, Louise hummed. "He's going to bid for the pearl necklace."

"You think so?"

"You just made the biggest natural pearl dealer in the world smile. That's a telltale sign."

Mad smiled and helped wipe the glass on the showcase. It was already 6:00 p.m.; another day of preview was over. "We're all set, you can go, Louise. See you tomorrow," Mad said as she took out her coat and bag from underneath the showcase.

Louise replied, "See you tomorrow," and strolled out.

Mad double-checked to make sure the showcase was locked. When she was certain, she walked towards the exit. As she walked out, she looked around to see if she would bump into Javier.

I didn't see him the whole day. I wonder where he is.

Mad could only see the Geneva specialists and helpers packing up for the day. Feeling a little disappointed, Mad left the preview room. She walked down to the lobby and passed by the massive display of flowers. The sweet scent of the peonies and tuberose permeated the lobby and uplifted Mad's spirits. Mad pushed through the revolving lobby doors and walked into a welcoming breeze. Closing her eyes, she felt in control again. It only took a few seconds, and when she opened her eyes again, Steve was standing in front of her.

"Steve!"

"Hi, Mad."

"What are you doing here?" Mad laughed. "How is it that we keep on bumping into each other here in Geneva?"

Steve grinned. "You feel better today."

"Yes, I do. There's no point wallowing in self-pity, is there?" Mad beamed. "Thanks for listening to me last night. You didn't have to."

"It was my pleasure."

"Are you waiting for someone?"

"No, I just wanted to catch you and make sure you were OK before I go. I'm heading to the airport now."

Astonished, Mad replied, "You were waiting for me?"

"Well, I don't mind seeing your smile before I leave," Steve chuckled. "You're much easier on the eyes than my secretary."

"Your secretary?"

"I mean, he's a guy!" Steve explained quickly. "And I'm going to be stuck on a long flight with him. Did I mention he snores?"

Mad laughed. "Thanks for checking up on me."

"I'll see you back in Hong Kong. I still owe you dinner," Steve said.

Mad corrected him. "And coffee."

"And coffee too?" Steve asked with his mischievous smile. Playfully rolling his eyes, he added, "Two dates, lucky me."

Mad burst out laughing even harder. Steve leaned in, and for a moment she thought he was going to kiss her on the lips. However, an unexpected group of Japanese tourists swarmed between them, and he stopped in his tracks.

Steve surrendered and said, "I'll see you back in Hong Kong."

"See you; have a safe flight."

Mad turned her back and walked towards her hotel. After taking a few steps, she looked around to see if Steve was still there, but he was gone.

▽ ▽ ▽

The day of the Geneva auction, Mad received a folder full of telephone bids from Asian clients. Her hard work had blossomed, and there was an abundance of bids. Mad even had multiple bidders on a couple of lots. Composing herself, Mad found a seat at the telephone-bidding booth within proximity of two other phones. She might have to end up using both at the same time during the auction. Seated next to her were colleagues from Germany, London, and France. Before the sale started, she asked each one of them to help her with lots with duplicated bidders. One by one she was able to find someone to help her out. Carefully, she wrote down the names of the colleague she would have to pass the bid to later, lest she forget in the heat of the sale. Right before Javier stepped onto the rostrum, Mad had it all sorted out and heaved a sigh of relief at what seemed like a busy but manageable telephone-bidding session for her. Mad looked at Javier as he walked up to the rostrum. Mad had not seen him since their dinner.

"Ladies and gentlemen, my name is Javier Rodriguez. I will be your main auctioneer today. Today's sale is placed in Swiss francs. Now without further delay, let's begin!"

I will show them I can do it.

Mad picked up her phone and started calling the clients. Everything was working smoothly, and she even managed to win a few lots for the clients. Lot by lot, she ticked off the checklist on her call sheet and passed her bids back and forth to her assisting colleagues. Things were on a roll, and Mad's confidence soared.

"Hello, this is Mad calling from Minos. I will be telephone bidding with you this afternoon. Today's auction is conducted in Swiss francs. Could you kindly let me know . . . ?"

On and on her calls went smoothly. Even Javier sneaked in a smile at her when one of Mad's telephone bidders won a lot.

That was before her call with Mr. Budiman.

"Lot 1450, a pair of sapphire and diamond earrings. The starting bid is at two hundred thousand Swiss francs. Mr. Budiman; would you like to bid?"

125

"Two hundred twenty thousand, two hundred forty thousand, not with us, two hundred sixty thousand, two hundred eighty thousand; would you like to bid?"

"Bid."

"Three hundred thousand is with us, three hundred twenty thousand, not with us; would you like to bid?"

"Hmmm . . . It's over what I'm expecting. Try once more."

"Three hundred forty thousand, sir. Still with us. Now three hundred sixty thousand against us."

"I'm not going to chase it. Could you call me on lot 1480? I'll try my hand on that instead."

"Sure, I'll call you back at that lot, Mr. Budiman."

Mad hung up and checked off her call sheet before proceeding to write in the client's name on the requested lot 1480. That was when her heart dropped. She had to call a bidder on that lot already! And a very, very important three-star client as well.

OK! Calm down, let's work this out!

Mad frantically asked around if anyone could take over lot 1480 for her but to no avail. It was one of the most popular lots: an extremely attractive pair of sapphire and diamond earrings by Cartier with an equally attractive estimate.

There was no time to contemplate her next move, Mad had several more telephone bids to call before lot 1480 came up, and she had to concentrate to make sure she didn't mess those up.

Lot 1460.

Lot 1470.

Lot 1475.

Mad quickly picked up the phone and called the three-star client, hoping that he or she would decide not to bid or even not pick up the phone.

"Hello?"

Dang!

"Hello, this is Mad calling from Minos, may I know to whom I'm speaking?"

"This is Sally, Sally Hung."

"Thank you, Ms. Hung, we are currently at lot 1476 and your lot is coming up at 1480, please hold on the line."

"Sure, thank you."

Mad quickly called Mr. Budiman, hoping that he might decide not to bid after all or forget to pick up the phone, but unfortunately, he answered as well.

"Mr. Budiman, your lot is coming up, please hold on the line."

Holding the phones in her hands, Mad looked paralyzed as she decided what to do.

Lot 1478 . . . 1479 . . .

Mad took a deep breath and snapped back into reality. She knew what she had to do. She placed the earpieces on each ear: right hand, right ear with Ms. Hung and left hand, left ear with Mr. Budiman. She looked ridiculous and most certainly got a curious look from Javier himself.

"Hello. This is Mad back on the line. The next lot is lot 1480, the pair of sapphire and diamond earrings, by Cartier."

"Yes," acknowledged Ms. Hung.

"OK," said Mr. Budiman.

Ms. Hung and Mr. Budiman were both clueless that they were talking to Mad at the same time.

"The starting bid is twenty thousand. Forty thousand. And now we're at two hundred thousand."

"Two hundred thousand already?" Ms. Hung and Mr. Budiman both shouted into the phone.

"Yes, we have a bidder in the room who just called out two hundred thousand Swiss francs."

"Goodness," Ms. Hung said.

Mr. Budiman groaned.

"Would you like to bid?"

No answer from either client.

"Two hundred fifty thousand. Three hundred thousand. Three hundred fifty thousand. Five hundred thousand. It's still not with us; would you like to bid?"

"This is absolutely crazy; bid six hundred thousand!" Ms. Hung screamed on the phone.

Mad froze.

Six hundred thousand!

"Five hundred thousand already?" Mr. Budiman quickly exclaimed. "It's OK, this is way over what I expected. It's almost sunrise here in Jakarta; I'm going to bed. Goodbye." He hung up the phone.

Mad's heart thumped as she instantly flung her hand up and yelled, "Bidding, sir! Six hundred thousand!"

There was a moment of silence as Mad slowly put her left hand down to hang up Mr. Budiman's phone line.

A room bidder finally screamed, "Six hundred fifty thousand," and swiftly took the attention away from Mad.

"Madam, six hundred fifty thousand, not with us; would you like to bid?"

Ms. Hung started talking in Chinese. *"Ma de! Laozi gen ni ping guo! Ba shi wan!"* Which loosely translated to "Fuck! I'm going to fight till death! Eight hundred thousand!"

"Eight hundred thousand, sir!" Mad said to Javier, trying to compose herself while Ms. Hung continued with a slew of Chinese swear words on the phone.

"Eight hundred thousand is with you, Mad. What say you?" Javier looked at the room bidder.

The room bidder pulled up his paddle.

"Eight hundred fifty thousand, thank you, sir. Mad?"

"Eight hundred fifty thousand is not with us, madam; would you like to bid?"

Ms. Hung screamed on the phone, and Mad had to hold the earpiece a little farther away as Ms. Hung amped up her swear words.

Mad looked at Javier and mouthed, "A moment please, sir," and used her index finger to signify that she just needed a moment.

Ms. Hung finally blurted out a comprehensible one million Swiss francs.

Mad took a deep breath, looked at Javier, and announced, "One million, sir."

Everyone in the room let out a sound of some sort and turned to look at the room bidder, who could only shake his head.

Javier faced Mad, slowly lifted his gavel, and hammered. With a smile, he asked, "Your paddle number, please?"

Mad lifted her paddle while everyone clapped in the room. "Congratulations on your successful bid, Ms. Hung."

"Oh, I am so happy, now I can sleep. Good night!" And click, she was gone.

Mad slowly hung up her phone as well. The New York representative gave her a pat on the back, and even the Germany representative who barely showed any emotions winked at her. Mad looked down at her call sheet and smiled at her triumphant finale. Reflecting on her week in Geneva, she knew she'd completed her task with flying colors. She felt good. She felt confident. She felt invincible.

CHAPTER NINE

A day after the Geneva sale, Mad arrived back in Hong Kong early in the morning. She went home and quickly prepared for the workday. Riding on cloud nine, Mad waltzed into the office and recounted her accomplishments. Not only did she secure multiple bids for their upcoming sale (even one from the largest natural pearl dealer in the world), but she also obtained an auction record for a pair of Cartier sapphire and diamond earrings, and that was for a pair of earrings without provenance!

Javier had been messaging her as well. Mostly just normal chitchat, but occasionally the messages were flirtatious. Walking towards her desk, she was abruptly stopped by the Boss's yelling.

"Mad!"

Mad walked into her room and closed the door behind her.

"I see that you have brought back many bids and interests."

"Oh, it was nothing."

"You know, Mad, when I look at you, I see such a strong woman," the Boss said. "You remind me of my younger self."

"I do?"

"Yes. It's hard being a woman in this male-dominated business. Every dealer is a crook, and everyone in this company is trying to topple you over. No one can be trusted . . . the higher you climb, the bigger the target you are—especially when you are a woman. Mad, we women must stand by each other. We have to help each other out, if not, who will? That's what we women do for each other."

The Boss continued. "I know you understand where I'm coming from, and I greatly appreciate you taking one for the team. The record mistake in the interview is already corrected on the online post. There is no need to worry about it." The Boss paused, waiting for Mad to say something.

Mad didn't say anything.

You threw me under the bus.

The Boss placed her hand on Mad's face and gently tucked her hair behind her left ear. "I see a lot of opportunities for you and a very bright future. Keep up the hard work."

With that, the Boss returned to her computer. It was Mad's cue to leave the room. Mad slowly headed for the door.

"Oh, Mad?"

"Yes?" Mad turned around.

"Smile when you walk out, please," the Boss instructed her and went back to her work.

Mad forced a smile and left the room.

As she walked towards her desk, the office door opened. An HR employee walked in with a girl so radiant, she looked like sunshine.

"Hello! This is Clarisse. She will be your intern for the next few months," said the HR employee.

"Hello, everyone! I'm Clarisse! I'm so happy to be here!" Clarisse beamed.

"So, you've all met Clarisse," the Boss said as she walked out of her office.

"Hello, Boss! I'm so glad to be here, and thank you so much for this opportunity," the little ray of sunshine said.

"Come into my room, and let's have a chat," the Boss instructed.

They both walked into the room and closed the door.

"That's Clarisse Kwok from the real estate developer Kwok family, you know. That's why she's working here," Veronica whispered into Mad's ear in disgust.

"She seems like a very sweet girl," Mad said to Veronica.

"Let's see how long she lasts," Veronica said as she flung her hair to the side with a swift turn of her hand, turned around, and walked back to her desk.

Good morning my dear

It was Javier!

Mad:

Good morning! How are you? We have a new intern here

Mad waited, but he didn't reply. This was how their interchanges were usually. Javier would send a message to Mad and make her heart flutter. Sometimes he would reply with a flurry of messages and sometimes just one or two. They were definitely not considered dating, so Mad just had to label him as a very friendly boss—in case he broke her heart.

He's probably busy with his work and couldn't keep on replying anyways.

Besides, Mad had work to do and a ladder to climb.

"Clarisse, you can sit behind Mad." The Boss directed the new intern to the desk behind Mad after they came out from their secret discussion.

Lugging her Chanel bag, Clarisse deposited it on her desk before quickly putting her hand out to shake Mad's.

"Hi, Mad! Please do let me know what I can help you with." Mad extended her hand as well to the polite young woman. *Something so rare these days.*

"Hi, Clarisse, welcome to the team," Mad replied. "I'm not sure what you can help me with at the moment, but I'll let you know if anything comes up."

There was a look of disappointment on Clarisse's face, as if Mad had squashed her eagerness.

Fresh graduates.

Feeling a little bad for extinguishing Clarisse's sunshine, Mad asked, "What are you doing for lunch today; maybe we can go grab something together?"

Clarisse's eye lit up. "Sure!"

Mad sat back down at her desk. She turned to the front of the room and saw heads turning quickly back to their computer screens.

▽   ▽   ▽

As promised, Mad brought Clarisse out for lunch. The girl was an open book! Clarisse told Mad about her wealthy family background, how she got the internship through her family connections but was here to prove that she was up for the job. She'd just graduated from college, majored in art history, and planned to take the GIA Graduate Gemologist course soon so she could excel in the industry. She told Mad everything, and her laugh was infectious. She even talked about her ex!

"I had a boyfriend, but we are currently on a break. I want to explore what options are out there. If I don't do it now, I would never get it out of my system! You know what it's like for a woman."

She's such a happy spirit. I hope she doesn't get tainted. Especially with how Veronica and the others are treating her already.

After lunch, they went back to the office. As they settled down, the Boss told the team that Clarisse was to be given simple tasks that "did not tire her" and that the team should treat her "nicely." As such, she was given the highly important yet neglected job of alphabetizing the books in the jewelry library, photocopying, sending out auction catalogues to clients, and all the coffee runs.

She actively sought out work from the girls but was always turned down. Mad didn't have anything for her to help with, but she would check up on Clarisse to make sure she was all right.

"How are you doing with the catalogues?" Mad asked.

"Oh!" said Clarisse as she used all her strength to lift a few catalogues from a cardboard box and place them on her desk. "It's going OK! These catalogues are heavy," Clarisse replied. "I just need to fill out all these FedEx forms, but Ronald said he'll help me carry them downstairs to the front desk and have them mailed. That's so chivalrous of him."

"Oh, is that right?"

Ronald helping? That's a first.

"Do you have any clients you would like the catalogue FedExed to?" Clarisse asked. "I'm sending a few to my mom's friends who might be interested in a few lots in this coming sale. I can fill out the form for you too."

"Oh, don't worry about it. Just let me know if you have any questions with anything."

"Sure! Thanks, Mad!"

Mad thought it was quite strange that Ronald, all of sudden, was so selfless. He could barely lift a few bottles of beer, let alone a stack of five-hundred-page catalogues.

Doesn't he have to stalk the Boss or some other client?

That was when Mad realized Ronald was wandering, circling around Clarisse's desk, eyes looking down at the papers on top of her desk.

When Ronald saw Mad looking at him, he quickly said, "Hey, Clarisse, are you ready? I can help you move some catalogues now."

"Oh yah, I still have a few, but you can bring these down to the front desk first. Thanks again!"

"No problem!" Ronald said and scurried awkwardly out of the office with the catalogues.

He's trying to spy on Clarisse and steal her contacts. How despicable.

Even the Boss, who rarely left her room, took advantage of the situation. Before the first day ended, the Boss showed Clarisse the jewels from the upcoming auction.

"Have you ever seen a blue diamond, Clarisse?" the Boss inquired.

"Oh yes, I've seen a few aunties of mine wear them."

"I'm sure your mother has one too. What do you think of this one?"

"It's beautiful."

"Here, try it on."

While Clarisse tried it on her finger, the Boss added, "Ask your daddy to buy it for you! It suits you so well!"

Clarisse laughed shyly.

Mad didn't know what to think of the Boss's words.

Is she joking? Or is she for real?

Mad rolled her eyes, ignored the circus act, and continued with her work.

◇ ◇ ◇

The sale was four weeks away, and the stress level was increasing exponentially in the office. Other than being at her computer, the Boss was now constantly on her phone texting and talking, reminding clients to go to the preview and dissuading clients from buying something similar from competitors. Ronald and Louis were extremely antsy, nervous, and easily irritated. Equally tense, the girls avoided interacting with them. Mad minded her own business and stayed in her cubicle. Clarisse on the other hand, who had only worked for two weeks, was too new to realize what was going on. Her eagerness brought her into everyone's business and way. She was everywhere in the office, getting into conversations asking if she could help. They would politely decline her offers, but as the sale date drew closer, you could hear the politeness disappear and the stress increase. The girls especially did not hide their frustration as professionally as the boys. They probably didn't attempt to anyways and were happy to dismiss Clarisse from their conversations with a slight air of disdain—or was it jealousy? As the girls laughed behind Clarisse's back, Mad just looked at Clarisse and shook her head, mouthing, "It's not worth it." Clarisse would smile back and mouth, "Thank you."

Mad had not had lunch with her friends at the terrace since her trip to Geneva. They had been busy travelling and acquiring bids as well. Over their group chat, Susan suggested that they should catch up over happy hour drinks. All of them agreed that they needed a drink or two. Friday night came, and at 6:30 p.m. all of them arrived at Lily and Bloom, a restaurant with a bar that Susan and Liam frequented. It reminded them of the cocktail bar they would go to during their New York City college days and how they could offload their stress there. Lily and Bloom was a polished version of that cocktail bar, but nonetheless the establishment provided the mixologist drinks needed and a sympathetic owner who was always ready to listen to their stories. The bar was already packed when they arrived. They shuffled past the leather couches and industrial steel décor before finding a table at the back of the bar area, next to the enormous art deco chandelier. All four of them plopped down on their seats as if discarding a heavy load.

"What are you going to have?" Susan asked everyone.

"The usual," Liam said. "Old-fashioned."

"I'll have a flirtini," Mad said.

"Oh! Someone is feeling flirtatious tonight!" Susan exclaimed.

Mad grinned.

"What about you, Henry?" Susan asked.

Henry looked like he was miles away.

"Henry?"

Henry snapped his head up. "Oh, sorry I was just thinking. What are you having, Liam?"

"Old-fashioned."

"I'll have that too, then."

"OK, then we're ready to order." Susan waved at a waiter.

When the waiter arrived, she ordered. "Two old-fashioneds, one flirtini, and one sidecar."

She asked them, "Do you guys want parmesan fries?"

"Um," Liam pondered.

The waiter enticed them. "They're the best in town!"

"OK, then!" Liam succumbed and winked at the waiter.

"Great." The waiter grinned.

Once he left, Mad recounted her conversation with the Boss. She was so enthralled in the storytelling that she didn't notice the drinks arriving. "There was this interview that she told me to write for her *but* not to correct her numbers. Of course, I did as she said, and the numbers turned out to be *wrong*! The president wrote a hysterical email condemning the culprit, and guess what? Instead of telling the truth, the Boss wrote back and pointed the finger at me! And she had the nerve to tell me that we women should help each other and ordered me to smile when I left the room!"

"She just wanted to cover her tracks and play the women-helping-each-other card," Liam said. "You know the most important thing to her is her reputation."

"Yah, that woman would rather not get a divorce than hurt her own image," Susan added. "What else would she not do?"

"We have a new intern from the Kwok family, and you know what she's been doing?" Mad asked.

"Tell me, sister!" Liam said with his drink in his hand.

"She told *her* to ask *her* dad to buy *her* a blue diamond!" Mad yelped. "That was so awkward and embarrassing to watch."

"She's got to sell the sale!" Susan said. "You know the Boss has little regard for her moral compass."

"She has no compass," Liam stated.

"That's not right," Mad said as she shook her head. "I wish I could do something."

"Like what? While she's still making money for the company, the company is going to keep on turning a blind eye," Susan declared. "You can't go and tell HR; they're useless! You're just going to end up getting fired, ruining your career and life."

"That's too dramatic!" Mad said, lifting her glass.

"No," Liam acquiesced. "Susan's right. The Boss has too many clients. Too much leverage in this company."

"Henry, what do you think?" Mad asked. Henry had been silent the whole time.

"Henry?"

Henry looked up from his drink. "Oh! Sorry, guys. I'm just thinking about something. What were you saying?"

"I said, the Boss has too much leverage. There's nothing Mad could do," Liam repeated.

"You could leave, Mad," Henry replied simply.

"Leave Minos? And go where!" Liam asked, bemused.

"How can you leave the most prestigious auction house?" Susan added. "You can't go back to a smaller one."

"I can't," Mad agreed.

"Why not?" Henry asked.

"Because this was my goal—to be at Minos. My parents wanted it for me as well. People would think I couldn't handle the work. The pressure. I can't just go," Mad said.

Her parents had never said it, but Mad knew they wished for her to work at Minos. She had always wanted to as well. Who wouldn't want to be an employee of *the* market leader?

"Plus, I haven't even been here for more than half a year! That would look awful on my résumé," Mad explained.

"That's the predicament," Susan said. "Well, at least we've still got drinks to get us through. Cheers."

"Amen!" Liam said.

CHAPTER TEN

The weekend flew by, and Mad was back at the office early Monday morning. She liked to arrive at the office before everyone else did. It was quiet, and she could clear her emails before all the commotion started. Usually she was the first, but this one morning she wasn't. Mad walked in the office with her usual cup of coffee and pastry but heard someone whispering in the Boss's room. It was actually the Boss herself talking on the phone. Mad was careful as she tiptoed to her desk. The Boss was probably on an early conference call, and she didn't want to disrupt her conversation.

"You think I don't know?" the Boss snapped.

Mad had never heard the Boss so agitated before.

"With all due respect, I *still* have control over what the Lau and Ho families buy."

"I will have a talk with her; don't worry about that."

"Look, you deal with the board, and I will deal with the clients."

Slamming the phone down, the Boss walked out of her room and the office, oblivious that Mad heard her telephone conversation, or at least part of it.

Ding!

Mad almost jumped out of her chair.

Javier:

Hello dear

Mad:

You're up early! Is it 2am in Geneva now?
Are you just going to bed?

Javier:

I just got off a conference call and was thinking about you

We should go out to dinner again

Mad's face turned red. Thank goodness no one was around.

Mad:

Really?

Mad waited and waited. No reply.
He must have gone to bed.

It was a good few hours before Mad finished replying to all her emails. By then the office was buzzing with conversation and commotion. It was time for a toilet break.

Mad walked into the toilet and heard someone sniffing in the stall next to hers. It was probably one of those new girls working in the notoriously dog-eat-dog Asian contemporary art department. These art history fresh graduates joined the department full of passion and artist dreams, only to find out after a few weeks of picking up dry cleaning for the specialists that most of the time was not spent on work but on surviving the office politics.

I've got to get out of the toilet before I have to hear another sad soapy tale of vicious reality.

Mad certainly did not want to get involved. She quickly finished her business and rushed out to wash her hands. Unfortunately, the toilet door next to hers opened. But it was Clarisse who walked out.

"Clarisse! What's wrong?" Mad asked with concern.

"Oh, hi, Mad. I'm so sorry," Clarisse said as she blew her nose.

Mad quickly grabbed her some paper napkins.

"Thank you, so sorry. I'm so embarrassed."

"What happened?"

"Oh, I'm not the kind that cries so easily . . . but this is really . . ."

"Do you want to go home? I'll tell the Boss you have a family emergency."

"No!" she yelled. "Please don't tell her. Gosh, I'm so sorry you have to see this."

"Clarisse. Is there something I can help you with? Stop saying you are sorry; tell me what I can do."

"Oh gosh, thanks, Mad." Finally, Clarisse stopped, and they both walked to the fire escape stairs to avoid bumping into other colleagues.

"If you need some time, let me know, OK? Do you want some water?"

"Mad, thank you so much. You've been so kind to me." Clarisse finally calmed down, and tears stopped rolling down her cheeks. "The Boss had a talk with me this morning. I haven't given her my client list, and I haven't brought in any bids yet."

"What do you mean client list and what bids?"

"Well, honestly, my uncle warned me that the Boss would expect me to give her contacts or buy something from the sale. But you know, this is Minos! A world-class auction house. I never thought I would be forced to. She said if I still don't perform, I can forget about a reference letter and that there are tons of girls like me lining up for a job in her department."

"The Boss said that?"

"Yes. And that rich girls like me are all spoiled and privileged—but that's not me!"

The Boss is at it again! Clarisse is an intern; she's here to learn the ropes of the industry and the company. Wasn't the Boss afraid of angering her family?

Then it dawned on Mad. The Boss was talking about Clarisse on the phone this morning.

She desperately needed more clients! Is she losing her power over her older clients? The board must be pushing her to perform as well.

"Uncle Steve did warn me. I told him about you, and he said he knew who you were and that I could trust you."

"Steve?"

"Mad, what should I do?"

Then Clarisse's phone buzzed.

"It's Uncle Steve, wanting to know if I'm OK. I'm going to meet up with him for dinner tonight. Mad, can you please come too? I need to think about what to do."

"No! I couldn't possibly intrude—"

"Please!" Clarisse almost yelled again.

Mad realized that Clarisse's uncle must be Steve Lam, and she remembered how he had tried to kiss her before he left Geneva.

Does he trust me too?

"Very well, but promise to keep your composure at work today. You don't want the girls to see you like this, and if nothing else, do not show the Boss you're defeated. Being rich doesn't mean that you lack work ethics."

"Agreed!"

The afternoon went by slowly, and the office was particularly quiet. The air was so thick, you could cut it with a knife. Mad couldn't keep her eventful morning to herself and shared what she discovered with her friends.

Mad:

Can you believe what the Boss said?

Susan:

Of course. I'm so not surprised

There's talk in the office your boss is
losing her power over the big families. She
desperately needs new clients

Mad:

For real? But how can you treat this little
girl that way? That is so disrespectful! And
she threatened her!

Henry:

Mama's got to bring home the bacon! LOL

Liam:

PLUS Clarisse is rich. She'll always have
her family to fall back on. Girls like her can
afford morals

Henry:

That's so sad

Susan:

Welcome to the real world!

Liam:

That's life

That's life . . . if you let it be.

Clarisse left the office first while Mad finished her work. Mad didn't want to leave with her. Not because she was afraid of gossip or the repercussions, but because she wanted to hear what the whole team said once Clarisse was gone. Mad wished she hadn't, though; they were quick with their nasty comments.

"Did you see her? She just pretended nothing happened!" Lisa said.

"So embarrassing," Florence added. "I would just pack up my bags, go home, and cry if I were her."

Even Ronald chimed in. "Well, she didn't bring in bids. I thought she would bring us a list of new clients. It's too bad."

"She lasted longer than I thought she would," Louis said. "That's amazing for a rich girl!"

They all burst out laughing. Throughout the whole conversation, the Boss's door was kept open. When Mad left the office, she could still see the Boss typing on her computer.

Mad walked over to the restaurant and met up with Clarisse at the entrance. They were ushered into a dim room highlighted by blazing-red chairs and tabletops. The open kitchen showcased a vibrant array of fruits and vegetables. In the middle, the chefs stood in their dapper black uniforms, diligently adding this and that to the dishes they were preparing.

Steve was already seated at the table.

He said I was the only person Clarisse could trust.

"Uncle Steve!" Clarisse called out.

Steve gave Clarisse a big hug and patted her head, like an older brother comforting his younger sister.

"Hi," Mad said. It was at this moment that Mad had no idea why she decided to come along. It was obvious that the whole situation was awkward, and she clearly did not belong.

"I'm so sorry for intruding on your dinner."

"Not at all. I'm glad Clarisse persuaded you to come as well," Steve said. "I still owe you dinner."

Mad smiled. "And coffee," she added as she sat down.

"Or more if you would allow me," Steve said.

"With your busy schedule?" Mad laughed.

"Now you're teasing me," Steve said.

Oblivious to the flirting between Mad and Steve, Clarisse slumped down in her seat and narrated the whole proceedings of the morning. Mad had not heard the whole story, and it made her embarrassed and disgusted. Mad's discomfort must have shown on her face as Steve put his hand on top of hers.

His hand felt warm and comforting.

At the end of Clarisse's story, he removed his hand and agreed. "Clarisse, Mad is right; you have to go on your own terms. Your boss wouldn't dare touch you, let alone fire you, so get the experience that you always wanted for your résumé and go when it's time."

"Yes, you're right!" Clarisse declared. "I'm going to keep my head up and get my job done—show them my value. If I give them my contacts, I'm sure they will kick me to the curb! I'm not going to let that happen!"

"That's right! Now, let's forget about Minos and order some food! Waiter!" Steve called out. "Could you check to see if the champagne is chilled?"

"Thank you, next!" Mad said, smiling, and Steve smiled back at Mad. Clarisse finally let out one of her infamous infectious laughs.

All throughout dinner they talked and laughed. Clarisse divulged that her famous family, like most families, had their quirks and surprisingly extremely down-to-earth qualities; that was probably why Clarisse was so approachable and genuine a person. She talked about her dream of becoming a jewelry designer one day and opening her own atelier. Her uncle Steve had been the only one supporting her dreams, while her other family members just wanted her to come back and help with the business. Uncle Steve turned out to be Clarisse's mother's baby brother, hence his protective nature over Clarisse. Even though Steve recently took the reins of his family business, and from the constant buzzing of his phone was extremely busy, he still made time for Clarisse.

As their main courses arrived, Mad turned the attention to Steve. Cutting through her quail stuffed with foie gras, Mad asked, "So, what do you like doing during your free time?"

"You know by now I don't have much free time. When you see me at the previews? That's my free time. I look for jewelry that catches my eye, something rare, something beautiful, something different. It's something I can do for myself," Steve replied.

"If you don't mind me asking, what do you do with all the jewelry that you buy?" Mad asked.

For your girlfriend?

"A man's got to be ready."

"Ready for what?"

Twirling her *uni* and egg pasta with her fork in a spoon, Clarisse exclaimed, "For the perfect woman, of course! He's getting ready for family and kids one day. Unfortunately, Uncle Steve has not met the perfect woman yet. So, there goes all the fabulous jewels locked up in the safe."

Mad was relieved. She chuckled. "Turns out the safe is wearing the jewelry."

"You know, diamonds and colored stones are just stones made beautiful by human craftmanship, nothing more," said Steve.

"I agree, but there can be more to it, for example, provenance. Some stones talk to you, provenance gives it life. It's the person who wears it, the emotions it evokes, the memories that give it meaning," said Mad.

"Really?" Steve looked amused.

"Are you telling me that you don't think the Elizabeth Taylor collection was anything but ordinary?" Mad inquired. She went on, almost too enthusiastically. "The tiara that Mike Todd gave her because she was his queen, and he wanted her to have a tiara. Or the Taj Mahal diamond necklace Richard Burton gave her, which belonged to the Mughal emperor Shah Jahan, who previously gave it to his most beloved wife, Mumtaz Mahal. When she died, he built her the Taj Mahal! How much more love could be encapsulated in such a tiny piece of jewel?"

Steve smiled and replied, "You do know they had to cancel the sale of that diamond to appease an 'important buyer'?"

Mad continued without letting Steve's comment dampen her ardour. "Or the monkey necklace and earrings from Michael Jackson, perfectly illustrating the childlike innocence and playful characteristics of those two friends. And the charm bracelets?" Mad added. "They're not expensive or rare jewels but each charm has a story to tell."

"The ruby necklace Mike Todd gave her?" Steve challenged. "Ghastly gemstones, full of inclusions!"

"Yes, but she will always remember that perfect summer day, when she was just swimming, something so wholesome, and Mike gave it to her," Mad said softly. "Such wonderful memories before his tragic death."

Steve and Mad continued their debate on jewelry. Steve tried artfully to denounce the importance of a handful of historical jewelry pieces, while Mad described how each is beautiful and invaluable in their own special way. Then Steve would challenge her with some examples of the most highly sought-after stones in the market, with no story or provenance, just to throw Mad off, but somehow, she could manage to persuade him that there were stones with charm that were rarer and more prized. Their playful banter lasted for such a long time that Clarisse had to excuse herself from the table and go home.

Eventually, Mad made the last point. "I love tracking down amazing gemstones and admiring the expert cutting, polishing, and craftmanship that goes into the final creation as much as you do. But what really makes a piece special is when there's a story behind it. In my eyes, a 3-carat padparadscha sapphire could be worth more than a 100-carat diamond."

"You're not really a good salesperson." Steve grinned. "I'm going to need to have a talk with the Boss."

They both erupted in laughter, frightening the only other couple left at the restaurant. The waiter smiled discreetly before returning to his stoic facial expression.

Steve offered to bring Mad home, and she gladly accepted his kind gesture. They didn't talk in the car, but instead of awkwardness, Mad felt strangely safe and calm. As they walked towards her apartment lobby, the air was slightly chilly, and a soft breeze blew Mad's hair across her face. Steve gently brushed her hair aside and leaned down to give her a kiss on the lips. She slid her hand over Steve's neck and kissed him back, lingering in the moment.

"If you don't mind, perhaps we can go out for dinner again—just you and me?" Steve asked.

"I would love that."

CHAPTER ELEVEN

The next morning, Mad's alarm clock rang, but instead of belligerently waking up, she slowly rose from her bed. She smiled and headed into the bathroom to get ready for the day. The previous night had been a great turn of events, and Mad couldn't stop thinking about the kiss with Steve.

It felt strangely comfortable and natural—and perfect.

She never thought that she would meet someone, let alone someone like Steve. They shared a passion for jewelry and gemstones and could talk all day about it. He was compassionate, kind, and wise. He had turned up at important moments to support her and give her sound advice. Most importantly, he listened to her, and Mad was falling for him.

Mad couldn't stop thinking about Steve, and the constant smile on her face displayed her emotions openly.

She walked into the office and saw Clarisse already sitting at her desk.

Clarisse shot her a smile. She was ready to show everyone that she was here to stay.

Clarisse:

> I was the first in this morning! Can you imagine what their faces will be like when they see me?

Mad:

> I can't wait to see

Clarisse:

> I thought about it last night. I'm here to stay and I will leave on my own terms. I came to learn, and I won't let them squeeze my most important asset out of me that easily. They give me what I want, and I will deliver

Mad:

> I agree. Don't let them intimidate you

> Ding!

It was Jackie.

Jackie:

> Did you go out with Steve last night?!

Mad's heart almost jumped out of her body! *Oh my goodness! How did she know?*

Mad:

> It just happened . . . I need to tell you
> everything

Jackie:

> You better!

Mad:

> How did you even find out? I'm still trying
> to process what happened last night!

Jackie:

> I know everything. We're going to lunch
> today, OKAY?

Mad couldn't contain her laughter, and she knew Jackie must have had a friend of a friend of a friend who saw her with Steve. Jackie knew practically everyone, so it wouldn't be that surprising.

> Ding!

Javier:

> Good morning dear. How are you doing this
> morning?

Javier.

Mad's face froze.
I'll just reply later.

Ding!

Oh gosh! Another message!

Fiona:

> Hi Mad. This is Fiona from Geneva. Do you
> remember me?

*What a morning! All of a sudden everyone is messaging me
at the same time!*

Mad:

> Hi Fiona! Yes, how have you been?

Fiona:

> I'm very well, thank you for asking. His Majesty
> has a diamond he would like to auction off.
> Would you be able to help us with it?

A diamond!

Mad:

> Yes, of course! Could you please send
> me the details, images, and any certs you
> might have?

Fiona instantly messaged her images of the stone followed by certificates. It was a 2-carat heart-shaped diamond in fancy red color. The rarest color for colored diamonds in the world. Period. Many rose, purplish reds, or brownish reds had been offered for sale before, but a bloodred diamond was a first. Red diamonds were the only diamond color graded without a prefix of *intense* or *vivid* from the GIA, therefore, fancy red was the highest saturation possible for a red diamond; moreover, this diamond was cut perfectly as a heart! The ultimate symbol of love. How appropriate.

Mad:

> Fiona! This is magnificent! How much is
> His Majesty asking for this diamond? I'll go
> confirm with the Boss.

Fiona:

> His Majesty is looking for an estimate of
> US$4-6 million. But we're sure it will end up
> selling a few times over the high estimate

Mad:

> Let me get back to you. Thank you so
> much for consigning this beautiful diamond
> at Minos!

Fiona:

> My dear, we can consign it anywhere. But
> it's not the auction house that is the most
> important, it's the people we work with. I
> know we can trust you

Mad was speechless and felt incredibly honoured that the prince of Qatar would consign such an important stone to Minos just because of their chance meeting in Geneva. Who would have thought helping someone pick up papers in the middle of the street would lead to possibly one of the most important consignments in Minos's history? Looking at her database, what they were asking for sounded quite reasonable.

Bringing her phone, Mad walked confidently into the Boss's office.

"Boss, I have something to show you. It's a consignment I just got; would you like it in our sale?"

The Boss looked up from her desk. Mad brought her phone over and showed her the images of the red diamond and the GIA certificate copies.

"The diamond looks good, and the certificates are new. The owner is asking for US dollars, four to six mil."

The Boss's eyes widened, and she quickly demanded, "Who is the owner?"

"One of the princes of Qatar."

In a tone of disbelief, she asked, "Why did he contact you?"

As a matter of fact, the volume of her voice increased so much that people outside stopped what they were doing to see what was going on in the Boss's office.

"I bumped into his assistant in Geneva," Mad replied. "And she contacted me this morning."

The Boss looked at Mad, but her expression was hardly readable.

Was she upset I didn't tell her about it?

The Boss's rigid facial expression finally loosened, and she said, "Have them send it to our office so we can have a look at it first. Let them know an estimate of US dollars, two to three mil would be more of an attractive price, but we can negotiate once the diamond gets here."

"Are you sure two to three mil for the estimate?" Mad asked anxiously. "The total estimate? That's half of what they are looking for. The past records—"

"Don't worry, Mad, we can always adjust the price," the Boss said, cutting her off.

Mad looked at the Boss, disturbed by her estimate.

Who am I to tell the Boss she's wrong?

Mad knew the Boss had dealt with countless consignments of such value and importance before and if there was someone who knew how to negotiate, it was probably her. But something in Mad wanted to be extra certain.

"US dollars two million to three million estimate?"

The Boss didn't reply but waved her hand dismissively before she continued typing on her keyboard, which was Mad's cue to leave again.

"I'll let them know now." Mad ran back to her desk and relayed the message to Fiona.

Fiona:

> My dear, are you sure about the price? Did you give me the price per carat or is that really the estimate? Between you and me, this is quite low.

Mad:

> It's the estimate. The Boss said the price is
> negotiable and that we can always change
> it after seeing the stone. Can you have it
> shipped to our office for viewing?

Fiona:

> OK my dear, I'll let His Majesty know and
> will ship the diamond over

Mad:

> Thanks Fiona!

Fiona:

> I trust you Mad or I wouldn't even utter a
> word with that estimate!

Mad was on a high. If everything worked out, she would
have consigned the most extraordinary lot for the upcoming
sale! What an accomplishment! She couldn't contain her joy,
and she could see the others all staring at her. Ronald and
Louis more so than ever, with disbelief in their eyes, and the
girls were typing wildly on their phones.

Clarisse:

> Good job Mad! Can you see them emblazed
> with jealousy? We should celebrate!

Mad:

> Thanks! I just hope it all works out

Clarisse:

> Even if it doesn't at least they all know now
> not to mess with you! You've got the prince
> of Qatar as your client!

Mad:

> He's hardly my client! But I'm so glad they
> would even consider consigning through me

Clarisse:

> You're being so modest! You're a superstar
> now!

And that was what Mad felt like: a superstar. The news of her potential consignment excited the whole company. Mad was about to make their upcoming Hong Kong sale even more important than the Geneva sale. If she played her cards right, she might also get a telephone bid for this crucial lot. Mad received several congratulatory messages. Peers *and* management noticed her and smiled when they saw her.

When she left the office for lunch, the girls at the front desk actually asked if they could help her with anything.

Ah, the power of social media. How quickly news spreads.

At 12:30 p.m., Mad walked into 8 ½ Otto e Mezzo Bombana, Jackie's favourite restaurant. Although the décor was polished, sleek, and chic, the waiters and chef always reminded Mad of the warmth of a family-run restaurant. Even better, the food was dependably delicious and fulfilling—a certainty in life everyone craved. Mad sashayed into the private room. Jackie was already there, with her sunglasses on, hands folded—which meant that she hadn't had a good night's sleep. Mad could also see a second cup of coffee sitting on the table.

She couldn't help but giggle, knowing that the news of her and Steve must have caused Jackie's current distress.

"You think it's funny? I couldn't sleep the whole night!" Jackie exclaimed.

"How did you even find out?" Mad asked.

"Someone saw you two leave Robuchon last night," Jackie answered.

"And you quickly assumed we were seeing each other already?" Mad said.

"Of course!" Jackie bellowed. "Steve is never with *a* girl."

"What do you mean?" Mad asked, mystified. "Not even at business dinners or lunches? Or even past girlfriends perhaps? He must have dated before!"

"Not like this!" Jackie said vehemently. "And anyways, I can't even remember the last time he was caught on a date; that was how insignificant the others were."

"Well, first of all, we were not on a date," Mad explained. "I was there with Clarisse, and he happened to bring me home."

"And?" Jackie bellowed.

"And—"

A waiter walked over to take the order. "Ladies, can I recommend the—"

Jackie cut him off and said simply, "Dev, we'll share the *burrata* cheese, schnitzel, and the fettuccine."

"And champagne to—"

Jackie gave Dev a look that could freeze hell.

"Compliments from the bar," Dev said before hastily leaving the room.

"Thanks, Dev," Mad said as he reached the doorway, where he managed to give Mad a wink.

"We . . . clicked," Mad began to say. "And then he brought me home. Everything was perfect. And we—"

Dev returned, interrupting Mad midsentence. He placed two glasses on the table carefully and then diligently poured champagne to the brim.

After he left, Jackie couldn't contain herself and blurted, "You kissed!"

"Yes, we did," Mad confessed. "He said he would like to see me again, and I told him that I would like that very much. But, you know, he hasn't even called me yet."

"I've known Steve since I was five years old," Jackie said. "He doesn't just date, and he's not careless. Frankly, I don't mind you seeing him. He's an honest guy. I can tell he likes you very much, and from the sound of it, he's been smitten for a while . . . You've seen him elsewhere?" Jackie's eyes widened.

"Recently? At your party, remember? And I bumped into him in Geneva during the sales. We had a drink and chatted at the bar. He told me to be careful of my boss."

"As you should—your boss's reputation precedes her."

"That's what many—"

"Enough about her. She's the least of my concerns. What else?"

"What else? About Steve? He hasn't even called or messaged yet. I think you're putting way too much emphasis on what's going on or *not* going on!" Mad said with disappointment, but almost immediately her phone sounded.

Ding!

It was Steve.

Steve:

> Congratulations on your red diamond consignment
>
> I'm so sorry I didn't message you this morning
>
> Are you free tonight?

Mad's heart skipped a beat. She started typing a message but quickly deleted it.
I'm not sure what to write!
Every sense in her told Mad to say no, she wasn't free. It was basic dating 101, you never say yes to dates on such short notice, even if you really want to.

Steve:

> Please forgive me for the haste . . . it's just that I can't stop thinking about you

Mad's heart leapt out of her body! She wasn't sure how many more times her heart could handle such shock. She was about to finish typing her response when Steve sent her another message.

Steve:

> I know I must sound like an idiot!
>
> I understand if you already have plans.
> Do let me know if you are perhaps free
> another day?

Mad let out a big sigh; the frown on her face dissipated, and a smile took its place. She deleted what she had typed, wrote what she wanted to say, and sent her message to Steve.

Mad:

> I would very much love to see you tonight.
> I've been thinking about you as well

She didn't need to say anything more. She was going to meet Steve tonight, and the feeling was mutual.

Steve:

> I'll see you tonight!
>
> Oh, and please tell Jacqueline that there
> is no need to put on sunglasses on such a
> cloudy day

Mad looked up and laughed out loud. Jackie had already raised her champagne glass for a toast.

"Was I right or was I right?" Jackie said with confidence.

♦   ♦   ♦

Steve was already waiting for her downstairs when Mad got out of work. Ever the gentleman, he opened the car door for her. Mad couldn't hide her smile. As the driver pulled away, Steve lightly put his hand on top of hers. "I hope you're not afraid of heights."

Next thing Mad knew, they were on a helicopter heading to Macao.

"Is this what you do for all first dates?"

Steve looked at her and smiled. "Can't I try to impress you?"

Mad giggled like a little schoolgirl as she looked out the window and enjoyed her first-ever helicopter ride.

Upon arrival, they were chauffeured to a yellow Portuguese colonial house up on a hill. A large camphor tree growing within the white and black tiles on the ground welcomed them with its strong aromatic scent. They walked into a restaurant with charming wooden furniture and plenty of Portuguese trinkets dispersed throughout the room. The head waiter brought them to their table at the corner of the restaurant. Mad couldn't help but notice how the smiling waiters eagerly served them.

Mad heard two quietly conversing:

"He brought a girl?"

"Really?"

"Chef would be so happy!"

With a big smile on her face, Mad waited to see if Steve was going to disclose what was going on. Yet, he was so focused on the menu he didn't hear the whisperings. That was when the kitchen door banged open, and out ran the chef.

"Steeeevvvveee! What have we here?" the chef said boisterously.

The chef was an elderly, chubby Portuguese woman who obviously was overwhelmingly delighted to see them.

"Mama Mariana," Steve answered, "I would like you to meet Madeleine."

"You can just call me Mad," Mad replied.

Mad extended her hand for a handshake but was given a vigorous bear hug instead.

"We do hugs here!" Mama Mariana exclaimed. "Now! Let me take a look at you!" She swung Mad around to have a better look at her whole body. Mad almost fell when Mama Mariana faltered, but Steve swung forward and caught her.

"I've got you," Steve said as Mad gazed into his eyes.

Ignoring the romantic gesture playing out before her, Mama Mariana bellowed in disgust, "She's so skinny! Steeeeevvveee, how can you treat her like that? Do you starve the poor girl so she can meet your peers' ugly standards of beauty?"

"Mama!" Steve refuted.

"I won't hear any of that. Mama Mariana will feed you what you deserve, my dear!"

Mama Mariana grabbed the menu, marched back into the kitchen, and gave Steve a wink—and a nod of approval.

Mad grinned and looked at Steve.

"She treats me like her son," Steve said warmly before joking, "but apparently she likes you more." Then he added, "Welcome to my world."

Mad was touched. It was obvious that Steve had brought her to a place that he held dear.

Two glasses of champagne arrived.

"To the rising star at Minos!"

"Thank you," Mad said bashfully as their glasses clinked and they each took a sip.

"You haven't even told me more about the red diamond. I might be your potential buyer."

"You just might be. It's a red diamond—obviously—as red as a Burmese pigeon's blood blazing-red ruby, but with the unmistakable lustre and brilliance of a diamond," Mad explained. "Fun fact, it's most probably the structural features in the diamond's crystal lattice combined with minute amounts of nitrogen that makes it so red. The most magnificent thing is, it's cut as a heart. This might just be the ultimate expression of love."

"Is that so?" Steve beamed while holding his champagne glass.

"As a collector, you know how rare a red diamond is. This is fancy red in color, the highest saturation possible and with no other secondary colors. This is rarer than blue or pink! What colors do you have in your collection?"

"You know what, I might just be lacking a red one," Steve smiled slyly.

"Show off!"

Steve burst out laughing, to the delight of all the waiters in the restaurant.

Throughout the dinner, they talked incessantly. They talked about their families, their hopes, and their dreams. Obviously, Steve was born into an über-rich family and had all the resources anyone could dream of. As stereotypical as it seemed, what he lacked in life were time and choices. As he'd mentioned to Mad before, gemstones gave him his space back, and he loved being enamoured by it all.

"Don't forget the provenance as well," Mad added as she dug into the salted cod and potato fritters.

"Eh, sometimes," Steve teased, then said, "I like your parents already. Your father is wise. Not a lot of men buy women jewelry nowadays." As he spoke, the waiter delivered their lobster rice, a healthy portion of suckling baby pig, sizzling garlic prawns, clams cooked in white wine, stuffed mushroom gratin, and grilled squid. Mama Mariana was obviously not joking when she said she would feed Mad what she deserved.

"At least I know what to get myself, rather than wait for a guy to buy it for me." Mad continued as she looked at all the food in awe. "But of course, like you, I don't mind what my parents have led me into. I've seen so much—so many incredible gemstones—as well as experienced so many unbelievably—"

"Horrible clients?" Steve asked.

"Yes, quite horrid! Maybe one day, when all this ends, I could reflect and write a book. Hopefully, people would find what I have to say meaningful and enlightening—or just plain amusing."

"I'm sure it will become a bestseller because . . ."

"Because?"

"I like how you have different views. How you are honest and genuine. I like how you tell me stories about gemstones, and I'm sure others would too."

Slowly, they inched in closer for a kiss, entering a world of their own. They didn't even budge when one of the unsuspecting waiters barged in to say, "The rooftop is ready!"

Bashfully, he added, "Oh, um, just let me know when you're ready," then rushed away.

They took their time finishing up their dinner, then Steve led Mad to the rooftop, where the waiters had decorated and lit the space with Moroccan lamps and candles. A two-seater swing was set up with cushions and a blanket.

As they sat down, the waiter said, "Enjoy the show," and left them alone.

Steve shot Mad a mischievous smile.

Next thing she knew, the sky was ablaze with fireworks.

"Is this for us?" Mad looked at Steve, amazed at the display in the sky.

"Did you know fireworks come in all the colors of your favourite gemstones?"

"You remember what my favourite gemstones are?" Mad asked, astonished that Steve remembered that little part of the conversation from the night before.

"Well, it's not hard to remember, but you do have quite a few," Steve began. "Fiery green for Chivor emeralds. Bluish green for Persian turquoise. Electric blue for Paraiba tourmaline . . ."

And as if by magic, the corresponding colors blasted into the sky.

"Oh look, here comes the smoke and wham! Velvety blue for Kashmir sapphires."

"You're such a nerd!" Mad exclaimed joyfully as she admired the explosion of colors.

"Here come the pinks," Steve said.

Mad said out loud one after the other, "Pink sapphire, padparadscha, oh, here comes a light one. Did you put a morganite in there?" Mad asked, amused. "No way did I say I liked morganite."

"We're shifting into rare diamond colors," Steve defended himself.

Each saturation and hue of pink diamonds appeared in the sky: vivid, intense, fancy, light, purplish pinks, orange pinks, and pure pinks followed by other diamond hues of blues, greens, and yellows.

"There's a small yellow firework for your 3.14-carat vivid yellow diamond," Steve said as he pointed at one small but brilliant blast in the middle of the exquisite chaos.

The finale was a tremendous blast of red hearts cascading throughout the sky. As the fireworks faded, Steve moved in closer to kiss Mad gently on her lips, cheeks, and earlobes until she finally melted into his embrace, and they drifted away into oblivion.

CHAPTER TWELVE

As the sun rose, Mad woke up in Steve's arms. He was awake already, clearly trying to be careful not to disturb her sleep. They both watched the sun rise, and Mad felt peacefully calm and safe in Steve's embrace.

This must be what love is supposed to be.

They flew back to Hong Kong on a helicopter. Steve brought Mad back to her doorstep, just in time for her to get ready for work. Before Steve left, he quickly held Mad in his arms for a kiss before taking the elevator down to the lobby, a lingering boyish grin cemented on his face.

Once in her apartment, Mad rushed through her morning routine and rode on cloud nine all the way to the office doors. She was just a little late, but nothing could deter her from her high spirits. A hint of Steve's scent clung to her and brought flashbacks of their intimate interplay.

As she pulled her key card out to open the door, two security guards suddenly appeared, escorting Henry out of the watch department, a cardboard box in hand.

"Henry! Where are you going?" Mad muttered in astonishment.

"Hey, I'm leaving the company, Mad," Henry replied.

"What?" Mad asked with a shriek.

"I'll message you," Henry said before putting down his box and giving Mad a hug. "Bye, it was such a refreshing experience working with you. Take care." And then he left.

Mad couldn't believe her ears. She rushed to her desk and quickly pulled out her phone.

Mad:

Where are you going?

Mad waited for a few more seconds, but Henry still hadn't replied yet.

He's probably still being escorted out.

Mad quickly messaged the group chat.

Mad:

Where is Henry going?!!!

Susan:

He's going to Colux

Mad:

Colux?! Why?

Susan:

> Henry got offered a very good package

Mad sat still, stunned at the news.

Mad:

> Why?! How?!

Henry:

> Hi guys! Sorry for all the commotion
> and for keeping this a secret. I hope you
> understand. I am going to Colux. They've
> offered me Head of Watches

Susan:

> Congratulations!

Liam:

> So happy for you!

Mad:

> Why didn't you tell us? I thought I was your
> friend! Did you pretend to be my friend?

They all went silent, but Henry finally started typing.

Henry:

> Sorry Mad. I couldn't risk it and had to keep
> it a secret. I really can't go on with the
> amount they are paying me at Minos. This
> was the only way I can get a raise. I hope
> you understand

Mad did not want to hear it anymore and minimized the chat group window. She needed some time to calm herself.

He didn't tell me he wanted to change jobs. He didn't tell me he went for an interview. He didn't tell me when he got the job! I thought we were friends.

Susan messaged Mad privately.

Susan:

> You shouldn't be so harsh on Henry

Mad:

> Even you think I'm harsh? Has he been
> calculative like the others all along?

Susan:

> You know as well as I do that Minos does
> not pay well. The larger the auction house,
> the stingier they are. That's why, in Henry's
> defence, he must jump back into a smaller
> house sooner or later. There are other ways
> . . . but that's not something Henry would do

Mad:

> Like what?

Susan:

> Kickbacks from vendors! Bribes, graft, red
> pockets—all under the table!

Mad closed her eyes and exhaled.
Did I make a mistake coming to Minos?
Mad messaged Steve and relayed all that happened in the
morning. After Mad finished, Steve replied.

Steve:

> Would you have told Henry if you were
> given an offer at another auction house?

Mad:

> Of course I would!

Steve:

> But you would have risked being found out
> and jeopardized your future. I think Henry
> wanted to tell you, but he couldn't. He has
> his own priorities too.
>
> Plus, it's true, your department is famous
> for some questionable dealings. Your

boss is known for running a tight ship.
Perhaps other departments are the same
too. People have to find other sources of
income . . . do you even get commission?

Mad:

No

Steve:

Thought so

Mad flipped her phone over.
I can't deal with this. I need to calm down.
But within minutes Mad's phone alerted her to a slew of
incoming messages.

Ding!

Ding!

Ding!

Ding!

The girls started to stare at Mad. Mad finally turned her
phone over to see what Steve had written, but the messages
were from Fiona.

Fiona:

> Are you there?

Fiona:

> We need to talk

Fiona:

> ASAP

Fiona:

> Did you know your boss called to clarify the price?

What?

Mad:

> What do you mean?

Fiona:

> She gave us new estimates
>
> She said you gave us wrong estimates

Mad:

> What?! She gave me the estimates

Fiona:

>She called the Prince last night and told him you gave us per carat prices.

>That you wrote "estimate" accidentally

Mad:

>You're kidding me! I double checked with her

Fiona:

>I'm sorry Mad. The Prince has decided not to consign the red diamond

Mad:

>No . . .

Fiona:

>I'm so sorry . . . I believe you

>It's not your mistake

>But we don't tolerate deceit

Mad:

>I don't know what to say

Fiona:

Mad, as a friend, be careful of your boss

You flew too close to the sun

The morning had turned for the worst. Mad felt the blood drain from her face. She needed some clarification. Mad slowly walked to the Boss's door and knocked.

"May I speak to you for a moment?"

The Boss continued typing on her computer, noticeably ignoring Mad. Her scrawny fingers kept moving up and down without ceasing.

Instead of clamming up and backing down, Mad walked in and closed the door behind her.

"Did you call the prince last night and give him new estimates?" Mad asked while trying to control her anger.

The Boss finally looked up from her desk. "I've known the prince for years. We chat from time to time."

"And you told them that I accidentally gave them the price per carat but labelled it as the estimate for the red diamond?"

"Mad, in this industry, for big important stones, we give price per carat and not the estimate."

"I understand! That was why I asked you to verify." Mad could hear the anger amplifying her voice.

"Mad, if there was a confusion about the pricing, you should have asked me. It was good that I called and touched based with the prince, or they would be so offended at what you offered them."

This time Mad didn't even bother to control the anguish in her voice. "I did ask you, again because I was questioning your appraisal. You ignored me. You told me specifically not to worry and that we could always change the price later."

"Mad, I'm sorry that you were confused. However, I don't think you should let your emotions affect your professionalism. What is done is done. Now would you excuse me?"

Mad was in utter disbelief.

She screwed me up! She screwed me up on purpose!

Mad turned around. As she lifted her hand to open the door, the Boss reminded her, "Mad, don't forget to smile when you leave the room. Don't let your emotions affect the team."

When Mad walked out, everyone was staring at her. They'd either heard what Mad said in the room, or they all guessed it. Enraged, she walked back to her seat and slowly sat down.

Though she tried to calm down, Mad couldn't concentrate at all. She felt a breeze pass her.

It was Clarisse. She walked into the Boss's office and confronted her. "I heard the estimates you gave Mad yesterday, and she did ask you twice if you were certain."

Now they all swung their heads to the front of the room to see how the Boss would react. But she kept looking at her computer screen and blatantly ignored Clarisse.

"All due respect, you did say 'estimates' and not 'price per carat,'" Clarisse reiterated.

The Boss finally stood up, obviously angered by Clarisse's audacity. "Clarisse, may I ask what you're doing at the moment?"

"What do you mean?"

"You know, I cringe every time someone from a rich family asks for an internship here. You people walk in with your designer bags and privileged lifestyle with no regard for what it really means to work for a living. You're not only spoiled but also a burden on our department's resources."

"How am I a burden to your resources?" Clarisse asked with shock.

Clearly sensing it was his time to shine, Louis jumped in. "You're always late for work," he shouted.

"When am I ever late for work?" Clarisse shot back.

"Many, many times!" added Florence.

"What?" Clarisse cried out.

"You haven't even finished tagging the lots yet!" Veronica chimed in.

"You told me not to finish it last night! That they needed the lots for photography!" Clarisse defended herself.

"Please, Clarisse, no excuses." The Boss interrupted the screaming. "We don't tolerate such behaviour here. Do you know how many people would kill to work in my department? I don't think working here suits you at all. Perhaps you should consider resigning and returning to a world easier to handle."

Clarisse's face turned bright red, but she managed to fight off the angry tears forming in her eyes.

"Clarisse has never been late!" Mad offered in Clarisse's defence, but no one listened to her. They all stared at Clarisse as she walked back to her desk, clenching her fists. She took her handbag and, with her head held high, walked out of the room.

Mad stood as she tried to fully process this condonation of the Boss's behaviour and the outright perjury of it all. Everyone was back at their seats, and the Boss had already returned to her desk, typing away on her computer.

This is not right, and I will not let them get away this time!

With a surge of strength and bravado, Mad stormed into the Boss's room. "Clarisse has been a positive addition to our team. She has not been late to work, nor has she rejected any workload put on her."

Visibly furious, the Boss looked up from her desk, her eyes shooting daggers at Mad.

"Don't you dare shout at me!" she snapped. "The world is not fair! We are here to work, not argue about fairness. If I were you, you know what I would worry about? Your reference letter, your reputation in the industry, your future! Think about that!"

She's threatening and blackmailing me?

Outraged, Mad was ready to scream out the crimes and injustices she had witnessed at the auction and at the office. But she had to stop herself. Clamping her mouth shut, she knew a sudden outburst of condemnation would not benefit her at this moment at all.

All she has to do is make a few calls and that will be the end of everything I worked so hard for.

Mad's fire reluctantly extinguished. The Boss knew how to target her vulnerability, bludgeon her character, and strip her powerless.

Defeated, Mad walked back to her desk. She could see the others quickly pick up their phones and assumed they were busily broadcasting the drama that just unfolded.

Mad sent Clarisse a message to check up on her. But Clarisse didn't read or reply to the message.

◇ ◇ ◇

Mad woke up the next day and checked her messages; Clarisse still hadn't read her message. Taking a deep sigh, Mad got ready for work and arrived at the office as usual, before anyone else. The only difference? Mad felt sick to her stomach. Slowly, people started coming in, but Mad didn't even bother to make eye contact or say anything to them. She wasn't aware that the Boss had walked out of her room and started making a speech.

"It's been a while since I addressed the team. We've been through a lot of ups and downs these months, our tenacity and work ethic have made us rise up from all the odds. Clarisse has chosen to resign this morning."

You forced her!

"As upsetting as this news is, it's not the first time we hired someone of her background only to have them cave under the pressures of the work. We're built to conquer such hardships, and so it is with utmost pride that I would like to announce that Ronald has found a 34.65-carat fancy intense pink Golconda diamond for our upcoming sale. This will be our top lot priced at twenty million US dollars. Our upcoming sale is going to be the largest sale this season. *Even larger and more important* than the Geneva Magnificent Jewels sale."

Everyone started clapping their hands slowly. Mad could not believe it.

How did he manage to find a Golconda diamond? And a pink one!

"I would also like to congratulate Ronald for all his hard work these years. He's someone I trained very well indeed. Ronald is to be promoted to senior specialist, and all of you will report directly to him. Let's give Ronald a round of applause!"

They continued clapping their hands.

Ronald stepped to the front of the room to make a speech. "If it weren't for the Boss, I would never be where I am today. Your guidance, expertise, and patience are unparalleled. I may have found a 34.65-carat fancy intense pink Golconda diamond for our sale, but if it weren't for you, the owner would have never considered putting it in our sale. You are the true star!" Without embarrassment or shame Ronald enthusiastically applauded while the Boss looked on impassively.

Mad shook her head and continued replying to her emails.

◈ ◈ ◈

The nightmare was not over yet. The whole day was buzzing with people congratulating Ronald for his promotion. The girls were the first to rush over and shower him with endless praise. Louis told Ronald that they were bros. The endless phone calls from other departments congratulating Ronald irritated Mad even more.

Am I the only one not buying into all this crap?
Susan and Liam messaged Mad to check up on her.

Susan:

Are you OKAY?

This was bound to happen you know.
Ronald has been working for this position
for a long time

Liam:

He's working to be the Head of Jewelry one
day and he will do anything to get there

Mad:

How is it that people could stomach all this
fakeness and play along without showing a
hint of remorse? That is something I cannot
bring myself to do

Susan:

It doesn't matter. It's what people want to
hear

Liam:

Everyone's got a chip on their shoulder. No
one is going to play fair. Especially in your
department

On the other side of the room, Ronald and the girls burst out laughing.

"I know, did you see her face?" Veronica said.

"Gosh, she's so lazy, she deserves it," Lisa added.

"Well, girls like Clarisse are spoiled for sure. But with me around, I'll make sure you guys don't suffer next time when we have to take in another client's daughter," Ronald belted out.

Enough!

Mad pushed herself up from her chair and walked towards them.

"You've got all that you've wanted," Mad said directly to Ronald. "Perhaps have some decency and stop talking trash about someone who deserves more respect than all of you added together."

With growing fury, Mad barged out of the room. Her sudden burst of adrenaline kept her walking until she almost crashed into a stunned Ophelia.

"My dear, you've got to be careful!" Ophelia said.

"I'm so sorry, Ophelia! It's . . . it's just been a long day."

Mad walked slowly away, but Ophelia stopped her. "Hey, Mad?"

"Yes?"

"It's just a job."

"Huh?"

"It's just a job. Go get your work done and go home. It's not worth it."

"Thanks, Ophelia."

What does she know? She's just one of them.

As much as Mad wanted to treat it as "just a job," she couldn't let go. She felt physically sick and needed to rid herself of all the negativity in her body.

As Mad walked away, Ophelia shook her head and let out a sigh.

Mad finally walked back to the office. Upon seeing her enter, the Boss motioned her to come into her room.

"Mad, please check your attitude," the Boss said sternly.

"What? What do you mean?"

"It's been a recent complaint from several of your colleagues that you've been disrespectful, and your negativity is impacting the department."

"I certainly have not! Who said this? We can talk face-to-face and clear things up!"

"There's no need for such defensiveness. I'm here to tell you simply to beware of how you treat others. Now, you have an impending 360 scheduled. That will determine how well you have been working with your colleagues. *Reflect on the mistakes you may have made recently,* and consider your future with us."

Mad looked at the Boss, speechless.

When was this 360 scheduled? Just because of what I said to Ronald?

"So, let's be professional and concentrate on our work, OK?" the Boss said.

"Yes," Mad said begrudgingly.

"Now, Mad, please smile when you walk out," the Boss reminded her.

Enraged, Mad shut her mouth and walked out. She glanced at Ronald and his telltale eyes told her he was the one who'd complained to the Boss. They were going to use the *Prestige* magazine interview that Mad took the bullet for to ruin her future. Mad glared at Ronald, and he hid his face in his cubicle, avoiding further eye contact.

Coward.

◇　◇　◇

It had been a long day. By the time Mad returned home, she had a debilitating migraine and had to lay flat on her face on her bed. The threats, the favouritism, the backstabbing, the lies—it was all so absurdly surreal.

Ring!

Ring!

Ring!

Reluctantly, Mad picked up the phone.

"Hello?"

"Mad, it's Steve."

"Oh, I'm so glad to hear your voice."

Damn it! I forgot to return his messages today.

"I'm sorry," Mad apologized. "I forgot to reply to your messages. It was a long day, the Boss—"

"Why didn't you help Clarisse?" Steve said abruptly.

"Excuse me?" Mad said, stunned.

"Why didn't you stand up for Clarisse?" Steve asked firmly. "How could you let them bully and threaten her?"

Mad could hear the strained anger in Steve's voice.

"I tried to tell them that they had it all wrong," Mad started to explain.

"Obviously, you didn't try hard enough. I thought you were different from the others! But turns out you're the same; you're one of them!"

Outraged at how Steve was lashing out at her without even letting her explain, Mad shouted back, "If this is who you think I am, then that's who I am. I'm not the one who, on one hand, preaches about how diabolical the Boss is, but on the other hand, buys gemstones from the devil herself. Who's the hypocrite now? You're the one encouraging and facilitating this behaviour of hers!"

Silence.

It took a very long few minutes, but Steve finally replied, "The longer you stay there, the more you become one of them."

"Bye," Mad snapped and hung up the phone.

She was infuriated.

Not only do I have to take all this crap from the Boss and Ronald, now I have to take shit from Steve too? He's supposed to be on my side! Not even a benefit of the doubt. Did Clarisse tell Steve I didn't do anything to help her? Did she tell him that I was one of them too?

That thought angered her even more. She'd tried to help Clarisse, but she couldn't. Perhaps she could have done more, but then she would have had to sacrifice everything.

They just don't understand how hard it is for me.

Mad hated the position she'd been forced into; how she had allowed all this to happen by befriending Clarisse and letting Steve into her life.

I should have minded my own business. I should have concentrated on my career, my goals, and stayed on my path. But what would that say about me? I would be one of them. I am becoming one of them.

Mad needed someone to talk to. She called Jackie and told her what happened.

"Do you want me to withdraw my pearls?" Jackie asked Mad.

"No, no, don't do that for me."

"I put them in there for you," Jackie replied. "You think I need the money?"

"I know, and I thank you so much for it. But if you withdraw it now, it will make the situation even worse."

"Awww, Mad, I hate that they have this strong hold on you. You know if you want to, I can get you into another auction house—or even help you start your own jewelry company."

"It's so kind of you, but you know I can't accept your offer."

"You can lose everything, but pride is something no one can take from you. You know, you have to get hold of some evidence that they're price fixing. You must tell someone. Only then will you be released from this hell."

"I'll have to find a way. Thanks, Jackie; you've always got my back."

"I'm so angry at Steve! How could he even say those things to you! I'm going to call him and give him a piece of my mind. How dare he!"

"No! I just don't want to deal with him now."

I don't want him to know that I've been thinking about him . . .

"Very well, then, but so help me God, if I bump into him, he's going to get a piece of my mind. Your boss too—that bitch and her loser squad is going down. You know what they call these losers, pieces of—"

Jackie continued with her rant, but Mad's mind had already switched off. If she were to survive the coming days, she would need to close off and stop feeling.

CHAPTER THIRTEEN

It was a whirlwind two weeks leading to the next sale. Mad felt like a robot and worked in a trance. She only spoke when necessary and typically offered nothing more than an obligatory yes or no. Her every move was mechanical and on autopilot: press conferences and interviews for the pink Golconda diamond, calling and texting clients to come to the preview, packing and moving to the Hong Kong Convention and Exhibition Centre, setting up the jewelry in the showcases, and finally the obligatory pep talk from the president of Minos.

She knew everyone in the department was monitoring her, just waiting for her to make a mistake, mess up, and break down. But Mad kept her head up and worked stoically, independently, and professionally. Sadly, her passion for jewelry had extinguished completely.

It's just not worth it.

She didn't realize how disengaged she had become until the day of the auction.

A client walked up to Mad while she was standing at one of the diamond showcases. "Excuse me, could I look at the jadeite over on that side?"

Mad looked at her. She was dressed in jeans and a plain Gap T-shirt. No designer handbag or superficial signs of money. Mad rolled her eyes and pulled out her phone so she could pretend she was talking to a client. She turned to walk away, but it didn't feel right. There was an unease devouring her heart.

The longer you stay there, the more you become one of them.

Mad turned around and looked at the client. "Yes, of course," she said with a smile.

Mad led the client over to the showcases and took out the jadeite. Like an automatic prompter, she explained why the piece was special and how the price was very attractive.

"And if you would like to know what bid you should place"— Mad looked over to Louis—"our jadeite specialist, Louis, might be able to give you some ideas, right, Louis?"

"Yes, of course," Louis confirmed. "I do recommend the high estimate at the moment; there's been quite a lot of interest."

"See, I told you; you have such a good eye," Mad joined in.

The client looked pleased and walked over to the registration desk with a bid form in hand. Mad's smile dissipated instantly, and she promptly headed back to the diamond showcases.

She'd just started wiping away the fingerprints on the showcase glass when a familiar warm voice said, "Hey, good job selling the jadeite over there."

Mad looked up and saw Henry. She stared mutely at him.

"Mad, I'm sorry I didn't tell you about Colux. You're my friend, and I trust you. I should have told you. I just hope I can still be your friend."

Staring at her dear friend's face, Mad wondered why she'd been mad at him in the first place. The wall she had carefully built around herself crumbled as she looked at him, and a surge of emotions erupted within. Mad finally spoke with a heavy heart. "That means a lot to me. It's been a difficult few weeks."

"I heard from Susan and Liam. How are you holding up?"

"As best as I can."

Henry looked worriedly at Mad. "You don't have to stay here. You can come with me to Colux. If only you could give up Minos. It's just a name on a piece of paper. I know who you truly are, and people will know too."

It took a minute, but slowly Henry's words and the clarity of it all seeped into Mad's head.

It was just a name on a piece of paper.

Her burdened heart lifted. She no longer felt as if she were drowning, but instead she could breathe again. No matter what the Boss said, people who knew Mad knew the truth. And the people who didn't know her would eventually understand as well.

Henry reached his hand out, and Mad gladly placed hers on top. She could be free again. "Minos does not define you," Henry added.

I am who I am.

"Mad," Louis interrupted them.

"Call you later?" Mad said.

"Give them hell." Henry beamed.

Mad turned towards Louis as Henry walked away.

"Yes?" Mad said as Louis stepped precariously close.

"Mad, you know we could make a very good team," Louis said in her ear. "We did so well back there. Think of all the possibilities if we helped each other out in the department."

Mad look at Louis quizzically.

Louis explained. "Look, you're good with buyers, and I'm good with the vendors. I can get a bigger cut for both of us."

Mad gasped.

What?

"Mad, you might think I had a hand with Clarisse, but honestly it's not like I had a choice. She's the Boss, do you really want to get on her bad side?"

Now Mad was glaring at Louis.

"I'm not the bad person here, all right," Louis whispered. "I've got a family to feed. My wife is pregnant, and if I want to get a raise, I've got to play the game. Don't hate me for that."

Mad just stared at the monster in front of her.

"Mad, say something. What do you think? Partner? All you need to do is push the items I tell you to push."

Mad took a step so close to Louis she could feel his breath on her face. "Louis, look in the mirror. I'm not you and will *never* become you. Be afraid, because everything you've done will come back to haunt you. I promise you that."

Visibly horrified, Louis stood stupefied. With that, Mad turned around and left. She needed a breather. Walking as fast as she could, she left the preview room and then started running. She ran past the large auction room towards the atrium. As she approached the atrium, she heard someone call her. "Mad!"

It was Javier.

Catching up to her, he said, "Hey, are you OK? I haven't heard from you for a while. I'm worried about you."

My knight in shining armour.

Panting, Mad replied, "Oh, Javier, so many things have happened. Can we talk?"

Javier waved to the girl standing next to him with a pile of papers. "Let me come back to you." And then he gave her a megawatt smile.

"Come, let's go get a coffee."

"Thanks, Javier."

This was the chance Mad was waiting for. She could finally report the Boss to upper management and have her prosecuted!

They headed towards the VIP café where, fortunately, not a lot of clients were. Once they'd sat down at a corner table, Mad's floodgates opened, starting with Clarisse's story. How the team tried to use her, and when that failed, they slandered her, threatened her, and forced her to leave.

To Mad's elation, Javier absolutely agreed. He placed his hand on top of hers. "Your boss is walking on a tightrope," Javier said. "I'm so sorry to hear all these things happened to you. You should have called me. She threatened you too, didn't she?"

"Yes, how did you know?"

"That's just how your boss operates. We all know. Don't worry about it; it's time she stops this harassment. Minos is a corporation, not her little rat pack."

Mad was extremely relieved something was finally going to be done to put an end to the Boss's reign. She should have told Javier sooner! But something still felt amiss. An unease lingered.

Mad looked at Javier with optimism. "What are you going to do about it?"

Javier smiled and gave her an unexpected hug. "Don't worry about it. I'll have a talk with the board. We've known about the

Boss's abuse of power for a while. But this time she's gone too far, and we can't have her infuriating Clarisse's family."

Mad felt so warm and safe in Javier's embrace. She melted into his arms.

"Now don't worry. I'm glad you stood up for Clarisse. I'm sure you're the only one she trusts. Did she happen to give you a list of her contacts before she left?"

Mad froze as memories flashed through her head. The morning that the Boss had that call with the mystery person. Javier's message about how he just got off a conference call. The Boss tugging Javier into her office to talk to him privately.

The room started spinning, and she pushed Javier away. She looked straight into his eyes. "You're part of it too," Mad said sternly.

Javier's warm, gentle face faded slowly, as if a veil were lifted, to reveal what was buried underneath it all.

"All Clarisse needed to do was give the Boss the list, then none of this would have happened," Javier declared. "Come on, this is not your first job. You know how this works. Clarisse is from a very wealthy family—she will be fine. She's rich, for God's sake! No harm done. It's people like us who need to claw our way up. Is that fair? Not at all. But the company wants results. You're smart; you understand, don't you?"

Mad walked slowly backwards. "Son of a bitch." She shot him a venomous look and left.

▽ ▽ ▽

Furious, Mad ran and ran until she reached the balcony. She needed some air before she suffocated from the toxicity inside the building. Huffing and puffing, it was a long few minutes until Mad realized she wasn't alone. Ophelia was smoking behind her.

Her nonchalant expression caught Mad off guard. That was the last straw. Mad exploded in anger and shouted at her.

"You think you're all that working at Minos. When you peel that name off, all that's left is depravity and corruption. You want us to sacrifice everything for that? Integrity, morals, even love?" Mad paused as Steve's face flashed before her eyes. "So we can tell people we work at the largest auction house in the world? How ludicrous!"

Ophelia didn't move a muscle, not even a twitch appeared on her face. It was a full minute before she finally spoke calmly. "You're right, look at all the people working here. Do you really want to be one of them? Question is, what are *you* doing here? Is this what *you* want too? You have love! Why are you still here? *Go!*"

Mad was stunned.

Ophelia agreed with me?

"What? And you?"

Ophelia smiled at Mad, but it quickly dissolved from her face. She lit up another cigarette and took out her phone to write a message before shouting at Mad again. "Go!"

Mad ran back indoors. The rush of the sudden adrenaline, the forcefulness of Ophelia's words, and her own heart launched her in the direction of the exit.

I need to find Steve!

Mad had almost reached the door and was about to pull on the handle when someone grabbed her arm from behind. It was a client service officer.

"Mad! I found you! Here's your paddles. Your auction is about to begin!"

Oh yes! The jewelry auction!

The client service officer dragged her into the saleroom while explaining the multiple bids Mad had to beware of that were overlapping or too close to each other.

OK, let me just finish this auction and then leave. At least they can't fault my professionalism.

Reluctantly, Mad took her bidding folder and walked up to the telephone-bidding stage to her seat. She was sandwiched between Ronald and Louis this time. The Boss sat right next to Ronald. Mad couldn't wait to get this sale over with.

Javier walked up to the stage and gave Mad a glance.

Mad glared at him and continued slipping the telephone bids into her catalogue, marking the lots she had to make calls for.

Javier started with his introductions. "Ladies and gentlemen, my name is Javier Rodriguez. I will be your main auctioneer today. Today's sale is placed in Hong Kong dollars. Now, without further delay, let's begin."

I'm ready.

Mad was unflinching. She called the clients one by one and checked off her call sheet.

"Hello, this is Mad calling from Minos. I will be bidding on your behalf today."

"Lot 3055, a pair of jadeite cabochon and diamond earrings; would you like to bid, sir?"

Check.

"Hello, this is Mad calling from Minos. I will be bidding on your behalf today."

"Lot 3071, the starting bid is one hundred fifty thousand dollars; would you like to bid?"

Check.

"Hello, this is Mad calling from Minos . . ." Each time Mad said this phrase, she became more jubilant.

Soon I will never have to say this again!

"Would you like to bid, sir?"

"Um," the client on the line said.

Hammered.

"The auctioneer has hammered at three hundred thousand dollars."

"What! But I was going to bid."

"Auctioneer's discretion!" Mad said with clear resolution and hung up the phone.

Check.

The girls looked at Mad, puzzled at her sudden change in spirits.

"Lot 3136, a diamond double-clip brooch."

"It's against us, madam; would you like to bid?"

"Oh gosh, should I?" the client asked with uncertainty.

Hammered.

"It's hammered at two hundred fifty thousand dollars. Goodbye," Mad hung up the phone.

Check.

"Lot 3276, a magnificent diamond tiara. The auctioneer is starting the lot at two hundred thousand dollars." Mad swung her paddle up with a flip of her hand, signalling to Javier that she was bidding.

"It's Mad's bid. Thank you, Ronald. It's not yours, Mad; it's Ronald's telephone bidder."

Mad didn't even look at Ronald or Javier. "It's not with us at the moment; would you like to bid, madam?"

"Bid up to a million if you have to!" the client exclaimed.

Mad's eyes widened, and she looked up at Javier with a smirk on her face. "Bidding."

"Three hundred thousand is with Mad."

"Three hundred fifty thousand with Ronald."

Mad flipped her paddle ever so lightly.

"Four hundred thousand with Mad."

Ronald followed suit.

"Four hundred fifty thousand with Ronald."

And the bidding continued.

"Five hundred thousand."

"Five hundred fifty thousand."

"Six hundred thousand."

"Six hundred fifty thousand."

"Seven hundred thousand."

"Seven hundred fifty thousand."

"Eight hundred thousand."

"Eight hundred fifty thousand."

"Nine hundred thousand."

"Nine hundred fifty thousand."

"One million with Mad; what say you, Ronald?"

Ronald kept talking on the phone while punching numbers on the calculator.

"Is the tiara ours yet?" the client asked Mad.

"No, madam, we're still waiting for the other telephone bidder."

"Who's on the line with the other bidder?"

"My colleague Ronald."

"Oh, what a vile name. Vile man too?"

"Most certainly, madam."

"I see."

Ronald managed to pull a last bid out of his client and flagged his paddle frantically in victory.

"One million one hundred thousand with Ronald."

"They have it at one million one hundred thousand, madam. Would you like to try another bid?"

"One and a half mil," the client answered.

Mad looked over at Ronald's sweaty face. "One million five hundred thousand, sir."

The whole room clapped and stared at Ronald to see if he had any chance of persuading his client to bid once more. But he shook his head, and a disappointed Javier hammered the gavel.

"Congratulations, madam," Mad said to her client.

"Oh good. We can't have that vile thing win over us."

"Yes, you are right." Mad smiled as she hung up the phone and checked her call sheet.

On and on Mad accomplished each call with utmost confidence. Finally, it was the last few lots.

"Lot 3304, an extremely rare natural pearl and diamond necklace," Javier announced.

It was Jackie's lot, and Mad was on the line with the pearl dealer from Geneva.

"We shall start the bid at two million."

"Would you like to bid, sir?"

"Mad, let's listen."

"OK."

Lo and behold, hands shot up in the room, and several telephone bidders swung their paddles around to catch Javier's attention. People started calling out bids from all directions.

The bidding quickly went up to three million, and it wasn't stopping there. It finally slowed down to two telephone bidders when the bidding reached six million.

"The bid is at six million; would you like to bid?" Mad finally asked the pearl dealer.

"Let's go," he said.

Music to my ears.

Mad shot her paddle up.

"We have a new bidder. Six million two hundred thousand, it's not with you, Veronica and Boss," Javier said.

All the clients in the room looked at Mad.

The Boss raised her paddle.

"Six million five hundred thousand, not with you, Mad."

"Bid," said the pearl dealer.

Mad raised her paddle.

Veronica shook her head and put her paddle down, signalling that her bidder was out.

The Boss raised her paddle again.

"Bid," said the pearl dealer.

Mad raised her paddle to seven million two hundred thousand.

The whole room started whispering in excitement.

The Boss kept talking on the phone with her client and finally raised her paddle to a resounding "Seven million five hundred thousand!"

"Wow!" the crowd said in unison.

"Seven million five hundred thousand against us; would you like to bid?"

"Of course, who do you think I am?" the pearl dealer countered. "But wait a little, let's make your boss anxious."

"Bidding, Mad?" Javier asked.

The whole room waited anxiously for Mad's response, and after taking a big, long breath, she raised her paddle. The room was in an uproar.

The Boss talked even more quickly on the phone. She knew her client was losing interest in the pearls, and she had to try hard to push for another bid. After what seemed like an eternity, the Boss looked up and asked Javier, "Would you take seven million nine hundred thousand?"

"Of course," Javier responded.

"Seven million nine hundred thousand against us."

"Eight million, then," the pearl dealer replied.

"Eight million, sir."

The whole room clapped as they enjoyed the show.

This time around, though, the Boss shook her head and hung up the phone.

Javier looked around the room and hammered the gavel.

"Congratulations, sir."

The dealer chuckled on the line. "Call me Mr. Jain. I'll see you in Geneva again, Mad. Thank you for your help. Bye." And he hung up the phone.

Mad was happy. Eight million was way over the high estimate. She'd done her job well.

"Lot 3305. The last lot of the sale."

It was Ronald's Golconda diamond, and Mad had to quickly call her last telephone bidder if she was to make it in time.

"Let's start the bid at one hundred twenty million," Javier called out.

The client answered the phone in time.

"Hello, this is Mad calling from Minos. I'll be bidding on your behalf for lot 3305, the 34.65-carat fancy intense pink Golconda diamond. The bidding has already started at one hundred twenty million Hong Kong dollars."

"Mad?"

It was Steve.

Mad looked down at her telephone-bidding form, which she hadn't had time to do beforehand. Printed on it was *Steve Lam*.

There was so much she wanted to say to him—mostly that she missed him. But she couldn't.

"You're bidding on this lot?"

"Yes, but that's not important. I wanted to call you so many times and apologize. I've been an asshole. I'm terribly sorry for my behaviour. I believe you. I've always believed you. Then Clarisse called me and told me everything, and I felt even worse and knew you wouldn't forgive me. I'm sorry it had to be a telephone bid. I thought this would be the only way you would listen to me," Steve said as quickly as possible.

Mad tried to look composed, but her lips slowly spread into a smile.

Steve continued. "I've picked up my phone so many times. I wanted to tell you I miss you."

Mad's heart swelled with emotions. There was only one thing she wanted to say to him.

She cleared her throat. "I've mi—"

"One hundred fifty million with the Boss."

"One hundred sixty million with Ronald."

Ronald?

The Golconda!

Mad looked at Ronald and the Boss. They were the only ones competing at the moment. She needed to pay attention.

"The bid is now at one hundred sixty million; would you like to bid?" Mad asked Steve.

"Oh, yes, yes, let's get this over with first. Bid, bid, bid."

Mad was about to raise her paddle when she saw hand taps under the table between the Boss and Ronald.

The Boss raised her paddle. "One hundred seventy million."

Then Ronald raised his paddle. "One hundred eighty million."

That was when it dawned on Mad.

They're doing it again!

"One hundred ninety million with the Boss."

People cheered.

"Quiet, please. Ronald, would you like to bid?" Javier asked. Ronald shook his head.

"Mad, are you still in?" Javier looked over at her. That was when everyone twisted their necks to look at Mad.

"The bid is now at one hundred ninety million," Javier said. "One more bid and we've passed the previous auction record."

The Boss turned around and looked straight into Mad's eyes, the thick black eyeliner emphasizing those icy cold daggers of hers.

Unaware of the true drama playing out in the room, Steve said, "How interesting. I didn't think this Golconda would make it up to one hundred ninety mil. Mad, I've realized that it wasn't jewelry all along. It was you. *My* choice. So, if you think we should bid on this, then go ahead."

"What?" Mad was astonished.

"If you like it, make another bid for me."

Stunned, Mad swallowed hard. "That's not up to me."

"It's fine, just bid."

Mad kept her paddle at half-mast.

Now the Boss was blatantly glaring at Mad.

Javier asked again, "I have to rush you, Mad." As sweat formed on his forehead, his strained eyes pushed Mad to bid.

Mad looked at Javier, then the Boss, who was mouthing "Bid" at her. Mad slowly raised her paddle while the whole room stared anxiously at her.

But that was when Steve said, "Mad, I love you."

Mad's hand stopped, and she took a deep long breath.

The longer you stay there, the more you become one of them.

Gently, Mad's left hand put the paddle down. Simultaneously, her right hand hung up the phone. With all eyes on her, she slowly stood up, turned around, and walked down the steps of the telephone-bidding stage. Composed, she left the auction room with her head held high.

At first, she walked. However, her pace quickened as excitement consumed her. She felt extremely liberated and emancipated. She made a beeline towards the exit. As she reached the end of the exhibition hall someone savagely grabbed her arm. Stumbling backwards, she gaped at the Boss.

"What do you think you are doing?" the Boss cried under her breath.

"What I should have done long ago!" Mad blasted back at her. "You're pathetic! You're just an empty, lonely crook filling up that hole of yours with all the dirty money you could steal. You thought I would crumble, that I could never leave Minos, but I've got nothing to lose. Judgment day will come, and you better beg hard for that soiled soul of yours. With all the things you have done, do you think anyone would have mercy on you?"

Shocked at Mad's brazenness, it took the Boss a few seconds to respond. "I gave you a job in the most prestigious auction house in the world. I nurtured you, I offered you chances and opportunities. This is how you repay me?" the Boss screamed. "How can you do this to me? You've broken my heart!"

Mad looked straight into the Boss's eyes and said deadpan, "Bitch, you don't have a heart."

Mad shook off her hand and, without turning back, walked out the door.

CHAPTER FOURTEEN

It had been a few days since the auction. Physically and mentally exhausted from the last months at Minos, Mad stayed in bed. She slept and slept and slept. Now that she was unemployed, she could rest as long as she wanted to. The old Mad would have been breaking out in a cold sweat, worried about her future. But not the new Mad. She received numerous calls and messages from the Boss. Javier, the girls, Ronald, and Louis left endless messages as well. Mad didn't return any of them.

I no longer need to waste my life on people like them.

The messages did not stop until the day Ophelia called Mad.

Still in bed, she picked up the phone. "Hello, Ophelia, what do you want?"

"Hello, Mad. I wanted to tell you that I've been working with the ICAC throughout these years to uncover your team's corruption activities."

"Come again? That's not my team anymore."

"That's right, so if you don't mind, we would love for you to give us some information on what you saw while working there."

Mad could not believe what she heard.

"You mean, you've been undercover all along? Trying to prosecute them?"

"That's classified. Now, would you like to tell us your story?"

Mad sat up on her bed. Slowly, she grinned. "It would be my pleasure."

"Good. I'll be in touch after a little outing today."

Mad hung up the phone and jumped up in pure delight.

The following day, Susan, Henry, and Liam messaged Mad notifying her that the Independent Commission Against Corruption had turned up at Minos. The jewelry department was being investigated for corruption and bribery.

Mad smirked.

Apparently, Ronald was the first to break down and confess. ICAC had been in contact with her friends too, and they had been all too happy to provide as much helpful information as possible to facilitate the investigation. They also told her that Ophelia had mysteriously left Minos. No one thought she would ever leave the auction house, but she did. Something about a much-needed holiday.

Clarisse also left her a message apologizing for her disappearance. Turned out, she had enrolled herself into the SSEF gemmology course in Switzerland and flown straight to Basel the night of the incident. She said she wasn't going to let a bunch of goonies stop her from achieving her dream or waste time crying about it. She was going to come back stronger and better than all of them.

As a matter of fact, the only person Mad had no contact with was Steve. Mad hadn't messaged or called him. Initially, she wanted to calm down first and digest what happened, especially what Steve had said.

I love you.

Minutes became hours, hours became days, days became a week. Mad hadn't heard from Steve by then either.

When Jackie went to visit Mad, she asked, "Why did you hang up on him in the first place?"

"He said 'I love you,'" Mad answered.

"No! And you didn't say anything back?" Jackie asked, flabbergasted.

"I couldn't. Everything happened so quickly. He wanted to bid on the diamond for me, but I saw the Boss and Ronald push the price up, and in the heat of the moment I just—"

"You took back control."

"Yes, it became clear to me what I had to do."

"Mad, I'm very proud of you. And I believe in karma. One day their evil deeds will come back to haunt them—oh, and that's why ICAC is investigating them now, haha!"

"Have you seen Steve around or heard about him?" Mad asked hopefully.

"He left the country the night of your auction."

"Where did he go?"

"A couple days ago someone said they saw him in Dubai— with a woman—but it might not have been him. What would he be doing in Dubai? He usually jets off to London or New York!"

Mad didn't say anything. Her heart ached.

"Mad, do you love him too?"

Mad thought about Steve's smile, his laughter, and how angry she got when he didn't believe her. She thought about their bodies entwined together in a warm embrace.

Mad took a deep breath. "I do." Mad started laughing quietly while tears rolled down her cheeks.

Jackie hugged Mad, and she laughed too. "Can you imagine Ronald's face when ICAC barged into the office looking for him?"

"Epic," replied Mad.

They both burst out laughing loudly.

"Karma's a bitch," Jackie added.

♦ ♦ ♦

It took another full week for Mad to recuperate and finally catch up with all her messages. She had an outpouring of support and congratulations from dealers and clients. Most of them offered her a new opportunity. However, it was Fiona and the prince of Qatar who gave her the most interesting offer— something that would allow her to pursue her love of gemstones without having to compromise herself.

Fiona:

> We want you to oversee the Prince's jewelry collection. Essentially, we want you to make it one of the top collections in the world. You're getting free rein

Mad:

> You're kidding me!

Fiona:

>We can't think of someone better suited.
>Knowledge, experience, passion, and most
>of all, we can trust you

Mad:

>When do I start?

Fiona:

>I take that as a yes

Mad:

>Well, how can I say no to you. I can't wait to
>see what other extraordinary stones your
>Prince has. Especially the red diamond!

Fiona:

>That? We sold it recently

Mad:

>To whom?!

Fiona:

>Someone very persistent and persuasive.
>I'll tell you more when we meet

Mad was typing *When can we meet* but was interrupted by the doorbell.

She ran over quickly to open the door and gasped when she saw Steve standing there.

"Hi," Steve said.

Mad looked at him and uttered a hi in return.

With his mischievous smile, he slowly knelt on one knee and revealed in his hand a ring box. "If I'd known you hated pink Golcondas so much, I wouldn't have even bid on—"

Before Steve could finish the sentence, Mad threw herself at him, embracing him as tightly as she could.

"Is that a yes?" someone said from behind Steve.

It was Fiona and the prince.

"What are you doing here?" Mad cried.

"Oh, we wouldn't miss this for anything. Plus, we wanted to know if the buyer is satisfied," Fiona said.

Steve opened the ring box to reveal a blazing-red diamond, heart-shaped, set into a delicate ring.

Mad's eyes widened.

Steve was the buyer!

"How?" Mad asked Steve in disbelief.

"With all my reserves," Steve said.

Mad smiled before they embraced each other and kissed.

💎   💎   💎

"I'll have your necklace delivered to your hotel in Mallorca. Don't worry about it! Didn't I tell you to trust me?"

Holding her cell phone in her right hand, Mad replied, "Yes, you did, Mr. Jain. Thank you again for finding something so meaningful for me."

"Well, I can't think of anything else more suited for your special occasion than this from Madame X's collection. The only pearl more emblematic would probably be La Peregrina."

Mad chuckled. "Yes, Mr. Jain. Now, the prince is also expecting his parcel at the hotel."

"Yes, yes, yes, it will be there as well! Twenty-four seven security! Don't you worry."

Mr. Jain continued talking while Mad looked down at her left hand. The red diamond heart was glowing proudly on her ring finger. It had been six months since Steve asked Mad to marry him. Ever since that day, she'd been extremely busy planning the wedding and taking up her new job. She had been travelling all around the world, chasing precious gemstones for the prince's collection. Occasionally, she would see something different, something with a little story. That's when she would add it to her own collection, knowing that one day, the stories of her jewelry would be told and inspire people.

Sometimes a little inspiration is all we need.

"Where are you, by the way, Mad?"

Mr. Jain interrupted Mad's train of thought. She looked out the oval window, but all she could see was the blue sky, a few clouds, and a clear reflection of the bold red lips on her face.

"I'm—"

Before Mad could finish her sentence, there was a knock on the door.

Steve didn't wait for Mad's reply and opened the door carefully so as not to wrinkle the white dress hanging behind.

"It's time," Steve said.

"I've got to go, Mr. Jain. See you soon."

Mad hung up the phone and walked towards the doorway. She gazed at Steve and thought about all that had happened that year. From landing her dream job to literally running away from it. Throughout all the trials and tribulations, she'd grown and learnt to stand up for what she believed in. In return, she'd made new friends and discovered new meanings and goals. She had found a life partner who shared the same love and values she did. Most of all, she was proud of the person she had become.

Jackie handed Mad a glass of champagne as she entered the adjacent cabin filled with her friends.

Holding up their champagne glasses, Susan, Henry, and Liam cried, "Cheers!"

Clarisse yelled, "We've got ten hours before we land, now let's get this party started!"

Jackie added, "Amen!"

Mad looked at all of them and couldn't stop smiling.

ACKNOWLEDGMENTS

This novel would not have been possible without the love and support of many people around me. I am eternally grateful and blessed!

Thank you to a core group of powerful women who, throughout my life, no questions asked, have always been there for me: Angela, Christine, and Tina. Many thanks to my dear friends at Miss Porter's School for teaching me how to be a woman and stand up for my beliefs and values. To my wonderful family for giving me continuous support, happiness, and laughter. Thank you to the most generous Maryrose and Claire; I certainly would not have been able to go this far without your invaluable advice. To my friends in the jewelry and auction industry: thank you for nurturing and helping me throughout my career. Thank you to the formidable team at Girl Friday Productions for being so patient with me!

A wise woman once told me that life is like a wave, full of ups and downs; you can't control it, but you sure can control who you ride it with. My life has been an incredible wave, and I thank you all for being there for me.

GLOSSARY

360-degree feedback: Feedback from an employee's subordinates, colleagues, manager, and themselves for individual evaluation.

absentee bid: A firm bid placed by a client before the auction begins, confirming the client's interest and bidding amount.

Burmese ruby: The most sought-after rubies are from Burma, where the most highly saturated red rubies can be found. Under UV light, the rubies glow a red fluorescence, giving them the extra redness.

buyer's premium: The commission the auction house makes from the buyer. The charge added on top of the hammer price.

Chivor emeralds: Emeralds from the Chivor mine in Colombia.

clarity: The absence of inclusions and blemishes.

color change sapphire: A sapphire with the ability to change color under different light sources. Changes from blue under white light to violet-purple under incandescent light.

colored diamonds: Yellow and brown diamonds with saturation beyond the GIA Z color and any other diamond with color. Colors include red, pink, orange, blue, green, yellow, and brown and can be any mixture of these colors. The intensity is described by the GIA by faint, very light, light, fancy light, fancy, fancy dark, fancy intense, fancy deep, and fancy vivid.

colored stones: Gemstones other than diamond. For example, the "Big 3" are rubies, sapphires, and emeralds.

colorless diamonds: Diamonds ranging from colorless to light yellow. Described by the GIA as D to Z color.

condition report: Report describing the quality of the lot. Gives other essential information such as additional certificates or stones missing.

cultured pearls: Pearls created by artificially inserting a nucleus into the mollusc. The mollusc coats the irritant with layers of nacre and eventually forms a pearl.

emergency bid: The maximum bid placed by the bidder in case he or she cannot be reached, or the phone line gets disconnected midcall.

estimate: A price range that the auction house expects the lot to sell for. Gives buyers a reference bidding point.

feng shui: Chinese pseudoscience using energy sources to harmonize people and environment.

guarantee: A guaranteed minimum price auction houses use to entice owners to consign a work of art. The auction house and the owner may split the profit once the item sells for more.

GIA: Gemological Institute of America. A highly reputable nonprofit educational institution and laboratory. GIA certificates are the industry standard for grading diamonds. Its Graduate Gemologist (GG) training program is world-renowned and provides comprehensive knowledge of diamonds and colored stones.

Golconda diamonds: From the now depleted mines of Golconda in India, the diamonds are famous for their exceptional translucency. The material of the diamond is so pure and limpid, it's often called "first water."

Gübelin Gem Lab: Highly reputable gem laboratory specializing in colored stones.

Gurkha: Nepalese soldier in the British army. Nepalese guards hired for private security.

hammer price: Price at which the lot is sold, not including the buyer's premium.

highlight lots: Lots in the sale that are the most unique and prized. Typically a high-value lot.

high-value lots: Lots in the sale with the highest estimates.

IC: Introductory commission. A commission paid to the client who helps the auction house source the consignment.

ICAC: Independent Commission Against Corruption. Anti-corruption organization in Hong Kong.

in-room bidder: A client bidding inside the auction room.

Kashmir sapphires: Sapphires from a depleted mine in Kashmir. Famous for their velvety blue color.

KYC: Know your client. A process where the client identity is verified in addition to potential legal risks.

La Peregrina: One of the largest perfectly symmetrical pear-shaped natural pearls in the world. Once owned by the Spanish royal family and also by Elizabeth Taylor.

lot: An individual or group of items offered for sale in an auction. Each lot is given an estimate.

loupe: A small handheld magnification tool used to see gemstone details, usually at 10x magnification.

morganite: A gemstone in the beryl family exhibiting a pink to orange-pink color.

MTR: Mass Transit Railway system in Hong Kong.

natural pearls: Pearls created naturally without artificially inserted nuclei. With increased ocean pollution, high-quality natural pearls are extremely hard to find.

no reserve: A lot without a minimum price. The owner is obligated to sell regardless of the final price.

online bid: A bid placed by a client online during the auction.

origin: Where the gemstone was found. This is important for determining the value of colored stones. For example, with all else being equal, Kashmir sapphires are considered rarer and more valuable than Sri Lankan sapphires.

padparadscha sapphire: A sapphire with a hue range in color from pinkish-orange to orangey pink.

Paraiba tourmaline: Gemstone in the tourmaline family known for its electric-blue and neon-green colors.

Persian turquoise: Turquoise from Iran. Top-quality turquoise are pure blue in color with minimum matrix.

pigeon's blood: Rubies with a highly saturated red color from Burma. Often compared to the first drop of blood from a slaughtered pigeon. Considered the highest-quality color and commands the greatest prices in the industry.

price per carat: The price of a gemstone per one carat, usually in US dollars. For example, a 10.00-carat sapphire priced at US$40,000 has a US$4,000 price per carat.

Rapaport: A transparent-diamond industry standard for pricing colorless diamonds. Updated every month. Dealers and traders price their diamonds according to the "Rap."

reserve: The undisclosed minimum price that the owner is willing to sell the lot for. Lots can only be sold at or over the reserve.

saturation: The intensity of the gemstone's hue.

specialist: Expert in their respective field. The job consists of finding consignments, appraisal, obtaining bids for their sale, etc.

SSEF Swiss Gemmological Institute: Schweizerische Stiftung für Edelstein-Forschung. Swiss laboratory known for its expertise in colored stones and pearl testing and renowned for its gemmological educational courses.

tai tai: A wealthy married woman who doesn't work.

telephone bid: A bid placed by a client indicating which lots they would like to be called on, to bid on the day of the sale. Telephone bidders bid on the client's behalf.

top lot: The most expensive and valuable lot in the sale.

treatment: Colored stones are commonly treated with fillers and heat. Treatments enhance the stone's quality but lower the gemstone's price.

white glove sale: An auction where all lots are sold.

ABOUT THE AUTHOR

M. L. Wright worked in the jewelry auction business for over ten years, including the prestigious auction house Christie's, where she helped lead the Asia Pacific department to a Market #1 status for years. Expertly trained as a gemmologist, she has a passion for all things jewelry. She currently lives in Hong Kong with her family and spoodle, Mushroom, and continues to work in the jewelry industry. *No Reserves* is her first book.